FATAL THREAT

VALERIE HANSEN

D0003501

◆ HARLEQUIN® LOVE INSPIRED® SUSPENSE

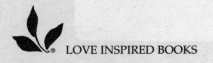

LOVE INSPIRED BOOKS

Recycling programs for this product may not exist in your area.

ISBN-13: 978-1-335-23191-8

Fatal Threat

www.Harlequin.com

Printed in U.S.A.

"When did you notice this damage?" Adam asked.

"What damage? What are you talking about?"

Grasping Sara's shoulders, he turned her in place, still keeping them within the shelter of the broad trunk. "This. See the hole?"

"We have worse things to worry about than a wormhole in a sycamore, Adam."

He was shaking his head and glancing from side to side as if searching for someone or something. Finally, he said, "This is no wormhole, Sara. The damage is fresh. And judging by the wood that's been displaced, the hole was probably made by a rifle bullet."

"Why would anybody go deer hunting in town?"

When he placed both hands on the tree, trapping her, covering her, she began to feel surrounded even though he was only one man.

Adam raised his clear visor and leaned in to bring his lips closer to her ear.

Sara was so nervous, so unhinged by his nearness she almost missed hearing him say, "They weren't shooting at whitetails, Sara. They were shooting at *you*."

Valerie Hansen was thirty when she awoke to the presence of the Lord in her life and turned to Jesus. She now lives in a renovated farmhouse in the breathtakingly beautiful Ozark Mountains of Arkansas and is privileged to share her personal faith by telling the stories of her heart for Love Inspired. Life doesn't get much better than that!

Visit the Author Profile page at Harlequin.com for more titles.

A man's heart deviseth his way;
but the Lord directeth his steps.
—Proverbs 16:9

Words cannot fully express my admiration
for the amazing people who daily risk their lives
to save and protect the rest of us. God has blessed them
with a heart for service, a keen mind and
the courage of David facing Goliath.

ONE

Flames were crackling, leaping and curling, their updraft sending sparks and embers whirling into the spring night from a burning duplex on the outskirts of Paradise, Missouri.

Fire Captain Adam Kane figured that the wooden structure was doomed. "Engine One on scene. Structure partially involved. Start a second alarm," Adam radioed before whipping off his headset. He grabbed his handheld radio as he jumped out, slammed his red captain's helmet down on his short dark hair and went to work.

"Clay and Walt, pull a two and a half. Peter and Rafe, the hydrant. Dave and Ty, to the roof. And get me more lights. We'll set up to force ventilate from the front doors so we can search for victims."

Besides the arrival of an ambulance, Adam noticed his own department's rescue squad slowly pulling through the crowd of spectators. John Forrester was driving. And in the passenger seat was lithe, blonde Sara Southerland, the ER nurse whose unexpected presence had unnerved Adam when she'd arrived at the station that evening.

Well, he couldn't allow himself to dwell on Sara's problems. Other lives depended upon him and his crews. Once the ladder truck arrived he could raise the snorkel and position it to spray the rear of the wood-frame building, doubling their efforts without endangering anyone. Or the equipment.

Radio in hand, Adam continued to issue orders. "As soon as the fan's in place, Walt, give me a quick figure-eight spray to cover the attack team. We won't have long."

Adam knew his firefighters were in full protective gear, yet he harbored more angst than usual. It wasn't that he was ever complacent about this job. It was simply an uneasy feeling that he didn't recall having experienced since ducking snipers and dodging IEDs, explosive devices buried in the ground overseas.

A quick glance proved that Sara was suited up in a bright yellow turnout, too, her sky blue eyes trained on the action. Was her mere presence enough to unsettle him? It never had been in the past, although considering the trauma she'd recently endured he figured he might have developed a heightened sensitivity.

Adam huffed in disgust. He was a decorated marine. A combat veteran. He'd guided men in battle and now commanded crews of paid firefighters and volunteers without hesitation. But one pretty volunteer EMT was enough to give him pause? That was not only disheartening, it was embarrassing.

Someone in the background began to cheer. Adam saw why and started forward to intercept his rescue team. The elderly woman supported between the men was unsteady but conscious as they handed her over to paramedics, then turned and headed for the second apartment.

Sara was gesturing and seemed to be trying to tell the medics something. When they ignored her, she turned toward Adam and waved her arms overhead. "There won't be anybody in that other unit," she shouted, approaching. "Vicki moved there right before we left for Texas."

Of course. That was why Sara had appeared agitated. Vicki's untimely death was still fresh in her mind and this had been her cousin's new home. Those kinds of community ties always hit hard and in Sara's case the effect would be even worse.

By the time she reached his side and stopped, he was already on the radio. "Be advised, that second unit is reported to be unoccupied." He was about to order them to withdraw when he heard another cheer arising from the crowd.

His crew had reappeared and were supporting the thin, limp body of a man. Adam frowned. Had a thief or arsonist been trapped by his own crime? It sure looked that way. He took a step toward the firefighters to see if he recognized the victim.

Sara grabbed the sleeve of his turnout coat so firmly she was impossible to ignore. He whirled, frowning. Her face had lost most of its color. Her always-expressive eyes were wide and filling with tears. Her lips trembled.

Expecting her to say something, he was jolted when she released him with a cry and began to run toward the rescuers instead.

Sara covered her mouth, smothering a wail. Unless her mind was playing tricks on her, she knew this victim. She and Vicki had met and befriended twenty-something Rodrigo Salinas while in Texas on their recent, ill-fated mission trip. The trip that had taken Vicki's life.

Gently cupping the unconscious man's cheeks in both hands, she raised his face to get a better look. It was Rodrigo, all right. Unfortunately, the rescuers had reached him too late.

A firm grasp on her shoulders pulled her back as paramedics moved in and took over. Sara knew it was Adam.

They'd been friends for so long that she could sense his presence without even looking.

"You know this guy?" Adam asked.

She nodded and met his dark gaze. "Yes. From Texas. He was part of the missionary project Vicki and I..."

"What's he doing in Missouri?"

Good question, Sara thought. Moreover, why was he in Vicki's empty apartment and why was it now on fire? What in the world could he have been up to?

"Good job, guys," Adam told his men. "Was that the last victim?"

"Yeah. He almost made it to the front door before the smoke got him." One man had removed his air mask and was coughing. A blackened smudge traced its outline on the sides of his face. "Looks like Miss Bessie was the only one to make it out alive."

Bessie Alt? Of course! Sara took a sharp breath and coughed as a result. Had she been so upset by the involvement of Vicki's apartment and the discovery of an unexpected victim that she'd missed keying in on such a vital detail? That was inexcusable for a firefighter, even a part-time volunteer like herself.

One glance at Adam told her he was clueless. His words confirmed it. "We'll take care of this, Sara. Go back to the rescue squad and get some O_2 to clear your lungs before you end up sick."

"No. Listen to me," she shouted over the surrounding noise. "I know Bessie Alt's medical history. She has a lot of breathing problems."

"Okay."

"Oxygen." She saw Adam tense when she pointed toward the duplex with her whole arm. "There must be tanks of compressed oxygen stored in there. H models, I imagine. The big ones."

"Everybody back!" Triggering emergency evacuation protocol with continuous high-low siren blasts he shouted, "Clear the area. It's gonna blow!"

Sara's mind was racing ahead. The instant she was certain Adam got the picture she turned on her heel and jogged through the police lines toward the ambulance.

"The fire department's bailing, Vince," she told the closest paramedic. "You need to load up and get out of here."

The shake of his head and slow laying aside of equipment confirmed the original suspicion that it was too late for poor Rodrigo. Sara gently touched Vince's arm. "At least you tried."

"Yeah. We got to him too late."

"I'm sorry." She sought to comfort him—and herself. "I guess it was his time to go."

He dipped dark brows and scowled at her. "That why you let your cousin drown, Sara? Did you figure her time was up, too?"

As unfair as his accusation was, Sara had heard whispers far worse since returning to Paradise. And she'd learned the hard way that rebuttal was futile.

She turned from him and started away, continuing until she had put a large sycamore trunk between her and the burning building. As she peered past the tree she could see engines backing up, repositioning. Only the aerial with the snorkel nozzle stayed where it was, presumably because it could shoot water from a long way off and still be effective.

Adam remained closer to the blaze than anyone else, shouting directions and gesturing. Her heart swelled with pride as she watched him. So brave. So capable. And so blooming hardheaded. What did he think he was doing? Didn't he have a lick of sense? Just because he'd survived roadside bombs as a marine, that didn't mean he was bulletproof.

She cupped her hands around her mouth and shouted at him. "Adam!"

He didn't respond. Considering the noise of the motors, pumps, sirens and yelling, plus the hiss and roar of the fire itself, chances were good he hadn't heard a word.

Every nerve in Sara's body was firing and misfiring. Her wobbly knees might have dropped her on the spot if she hadn't leaned against the stout tree. If only Adam would give ground!

What was the matter with him? Wanting to do good was one thing. Unnecessary risks were another. She ought to know. Not fighting harder to keep her cousin from behaving recklessly during the Texas flood had been her worst decision ever—one she would pay for the rest of her life.

Well, once was enough. If Adam wouldn't back off on his own she was going to drag him to safety, just the way she should have dragged Vicki.

Bolting from cover, Sara heard a distant pop and felt tiny, bothersome bits of tree bark raining down on her head. She absently swatted them from her hair. Her one and only mission right now was getting to her friend and convincing him to flee.

Screaming "Adam!" she dodged equipment and jumped fat, wet fire hoses that coiled on the muddy ground like seeping, writhing snakes. "Adaaaaam!"

He whirled. Sara crashed into him. "You have to leave. Fall back."

He grabbed her upper arms through the heavy canvaslike turnout coat she wore. "What do you think you're doing? Get out of here!"

"I'm saving your life!" Hearing herself screeching she

decided he wasn't going to heed her warning unless she made it more specific. "The oxy tanks. If they fall and the valves break off they'll turn into rockets."

"With a fireball on the other end. Yeah, I know." Taking one last look he pushed her ahead of him in a joint dash for cover.

Sara pointed. "That tree. Come on."

Rounding it, she flattened her back against the trunk. Adam joined her. Her heart was already pounding from the scare he'd given her. Now, it took off at a gallop. This was one of those extraordinary moments when she wasn't sure whether to weep or laugh. His handsome face was dotted with ash, smudged with smoke and his warm brown eyes were reddened. Nevertheless, the way he was staring at her was more than disconcerting.

His focus left her face to concentrate on a spot on the tree trunk directly above her head. When he removed one of his heavy gloves and touched the bark, more powdery bits and slivers rained down.

Sara brushed them away. "Stop that. You're making a worse mess than the first time I hid here."

His eyes were wide beneath the brim and clear faceplate of his helmet. "What first time? When did you notice this damage?"

"What damage? What are you talking about?"

Grasping her shoulders he turned her in place, still keeping within the shelter of the broad trunk. "This. See the hole?"

"We have worse things to worry about than a wormhole in a sycamore, Adam."

He was shaking his head and glancing from side to side as if searching for someone or something. Finally, he said, "This is no wormhole, Sara. The damage is fresh.

And judging by the wood that's been displaced, the hole was probably made by a rifle bullet."

"Why would anybody go deer hunting in town?"

When he placed both hands on the tree, trapping her, covering her, she began to feel surrounded even though he was only one man.

Adam raised his clear visor and leaned in to bring his lips closer to her ear.

Sara was so nervous, so unhinged by his nearness, she almost missed hearing him say, "They weren't shooting at whitetails, Sara. They were shooting at *you*."

TWO

Adam was ready to catch her if his frankness made her faint. It impressed him when she stayed firmly on her feet.

"What? What gives you that idea?"

"Logic. If somebody had had it in for police or fire they'd have aimed at our trucks and cars. You were standing behind this tree and nobody else was close by. Am I right?"

The fact that she simply nodded instead of arguing with him was telling. Hopefully, his sensible reasoning was getting through to her.

Her lips parted slightly and her fair complexion paled even more than usual, yet she was adamant. "Wait a second. I know what a rifle shot sounds like, the way it echoes and kind of whines. I did not hear anything like that."

"Then maybe the bullet was from a pistol. I don't know. I'll report it so the cops can dig it out for evidence."

As he spoke, Adam continued to scan their surroundings. His crews and engines were out of danger from the anticipated explosion. The telescoping snorkel was still pumping water on the rear of the building to cool it and protect nearby structures. There remained only one serious concern not taken care of. Sara Southerland. And a sniper.

Adam knew he could continue to physically block her if he had to but that left his own back exposed. Clearly, they needed better cover.

"We'll make a run for Engine One and hunker down behind it. You go first," Adam ordered.

"I'm not going anywhere without you," she said hoarsely.

That was all it took to push him to the edge of his patience. "Somebody took a shot at you. You can't stay here."

"Then neither should you."

"I said I was coming." Adam knew he was shouting at her but it was for her own good. He stepped slightly to the side and gave her a push. "Move!"

This time there was no doubt he heard it. The bang. The whine. The thunk when the projectile imbedded in the sycamore mere inches from his head.

Instinct took over. Adam threw Sara to the ground behind a cluster of low-growing bushes, pinning her beneath him and ignoring her indignant sputtering. This was combat. In his mind he was back in the desert, under fire. Unprotected. Vulnerable. And unarmed.

Reaching for his radio he shouted, "Shots fired! Take cover!"

Seconds later his radio crackled a response in his earbud. "I've alerted the sheriff," his dispatcher said. "That's not your only problem, Captain. Miz Alt has a prescription for two H tanks like you thought. One was refilled and returned a few days ago."

"Copy."

Adam shifted, raising himself slightly to give Sara relief. She immediately tried to wiggle away but he stopped her. "No. Stay put."

"I thought we were making a run for it."

"Not now that we know the shooter is still active.

There's no way to get to the truck without showing ourselves. We'll have to keep our heads down until the cops catch him or scare him off."

Adam knew they'd also need to wait until something happened inside the burning building. Either the tanks would vent or explode or act like horizontal rockets and take out walls. Maybe they'd do all of the above, depending on when the fire reached them and how they were supported inside Bessie's apartment. It was too much to hope they'd fall gently and withstand the spreading flames.

"Initial explosive hazard confirmed," Adam broadcast on an open channel. "All units hold your positions. Nobody goes near this structure again until I give the all clear."

Sara nudged him. "I was right?"

"Yes. Unfortunately, you were. As soon as…"

A muted crash was followed milliseconds later by a whoosh and sounds of cracking and shattering. A flaming, rolling, expanding ball of gas filled the duplex to bursting and sent splintered windows and walls outward while the roof rose, fell and disappeared.

Adam ducked instinctively. So did Sara. He covered her as best he could and stayed hunched over her until smoldering pieces of the destroyed building stopped falling around them.

A cloud of acrid black and gray smoke boiled from the site of the explosion, filling the atmosphere and stealing breathable air. It rolled over the scene like a malevolent entity that was bent on hiding the carnage and claiming more victims.

Adam's ears were ringing. "Don't inhale deeply," he cautioned Sara. "Fumes from burning synthetics can kill you."

"Or you!" she replied, coughing and choking.

"I'll be okay. There's plenty of O_2 on the engines. Wait a minute more, then keep low while you head for the squad. This smoke will hide you. Get in with Forrester. Stay there and keep your head down, just in case."

"No. I can help out here. There may be injuries."

"There will be for sure if you keep being so stubborn," he countered. "I can only do so much to protect you."

"I never asked you to."

"You didn't have to," Adam said soberly. "It's what I do."

Everyone's adrenaline had dissipated to the point of exhaustion by the time all the firefighters except the mop-up crew had returned to the station. Disappointingly, the duplex was on the ground and no sniper had been located.

Sara had given her statement about the deceased victim to police officers on scene, then ridden back with the rescue squad. The crews were done debriefing for the night, although their chief would later go over the primary attack on the fire and their coordinated efforts.

On-duty firefighters were cleaning and restocking the equipment and the other volunteers had left for home. Sara would have been among them if Adam hadn't specifically asked her to stay so they could speak in private.

Weariness made her mood less than affable. "Well? What's so important that we can't let everybody in on it?"

"You must know that better than I do. Talk. I'm waiting," he said flatly.

"For what? I'm as in the dark as you are about what happened tonight. Even if you're right about those shots, I can't lock myself in a closet and stay there to make it safe for the rest of the folks in Paradise."

"There's a lot more to consider than that and you know it," Adam argued. "I just want you to take reasonable precautions. The police agree. Nobody accidentally shoots the same tree twice in a row—while you happen to be standing under it."

Sara could picture Adam's larger frame physically shielding hers. By the time the second bullet was fired he might have been in the way. Therefore, the assailant had little concern for which victim fell.

"How do you know they weren't shooting at you?"

"Because I wasn't there the first time."

"You were the second time," she argued.

He grimaced. "Don't remind me."

Judging by his expression and the abrupt retort, he meant it. Well, fine. Sara chewed on her lower lip. *She* was certainly going to remember. The way he had protected her from both the impending blast and whoever was apparently threatening her life had brought back good memories. Sweet memories she had done her best to banish when he'd chosen to ignore her tearful pleas and enlist in the marines rather than stay in Paradise.

So, what do I have to do to get him to see me as a responsible adult instead of a giggly teenage buddy? she wondered with a sigh. Sara stiffened her spine, raised her chin and made sure none of the on-duty firefighters were listening before she said, "Okay. Suppose somebody is mad enough at me to try to shoot me. Who? And why?"

"Don't ask me. Ask yourself," Adam snapped back. "Start with why anybody would start a fire in Vicki's apartment."

"I don't have a clue. Really."

"How about that guy you recognized? You met him in Texas?"

"Yes." She swallowed hard, her mouth dry.

"What happened there?"

"Besides losing my best girlfriend in the whole world,

you mean?" She noted his morphing expression, unsure whether it portrayed anger or loss or grief.

Adam set his jaw. "Yes."

Sara decided he was struggling to control anger, which was actually a necessary step in the grieving process, so she tried not to hold it against him. At least he was staying civil toward her—for the present.

"Vicki thought she'd found a problem with the records kept by the local overseer for the mission organization," Sara said. "That was why she insisted on going back to the office trailer despite the storm. The Brazos River and its tributaries were already flooding and more rain was falling, but she'd stashed the proof back at the office."

He rolled his eyes. "That's ridiculous. She could have saved a copy on a thumb drive."

"Not without electricity and a working scanner to copy the original invoices. She—we—needed those paper copies. They had signatures on them. There was no way to prove who was involved in the corruption without them. Anybody she accused could easily have denied it."

"*That's* what she gave her life for? A bunch of paperwork?" Running his fingers through his short, dark hair he began to pace. "And you didn't stop her?"

Sara was trembling, inside and out. She clenched her fingers together. "I tried. She wouldn't listen. I told her the flood water was getting too high, moving too fast, but she was determined."

"You could have grabbed her, shaken some sense into her."

"I did!" Gulping back sobs Sara relived that terrible evening in a flash. "I was holding on to her slicker. It was wet. My hand slipped." She inhaled shakily. "And then she was gone."

Watching Adam's reaction, Sara realized he was accepting her story. When he said, "I'm sorry, but at least that explains a few things," she arched an eyebrow and stared, waiting for him to go on.

"I got texts from Vicki the evening she disappeared." He plopped down on the wide rear bumper of his engine, leaned his elbows on his knees and bowed his head.

"When?" Sara cautiously joined him.

"Around six. It was already dark here so the sun would have been setting where you were, too. She told me you two were okay, then mentioned the mystery game we used to play when we were kids. The game where one of you pretended to be Holmes and the other one Watson."

"That's it? That's all?"

"Pretty much," Adam said with a sigh. "I texted back for details but she never replied."

Mirroring his pose, Sara nevertheless kept her distance. The chrome platform of the bumper was cold, even through heavy fire-protective clothing. "That must have been right before she put on her rain gear and headed outside." An icy shiver zinged up her spine. Had the influence of Vicki's discovery followed her all the way home to Missouri?

"Maybe whoever was shooting at me thinks I can expose that crime. Vicki and I were always together. How would they know I can't prove a thing?"

Turning slightly to face her, Adam scowled. "The only way they would was if Vicki had told them so and they'd believed her. And that's only plausible if she didn't drown before…"

Wide-eyed, Sara pivoted to stare back at him. "Before?"

His jaw muscles worked as if he could barely make himself speak. "Before they had a chance to kill her."

"That is *so* not funny."

"It wasn't meant to be."

"Vicki drowned accidentally. The coroner signed off on her death without question."

"Because he was sure or because he was buried in work? No pun intended."

"You were at her funeral. You saw her, same as I did. There wasn't a mark on her." Sara's voice broke and she had to pause to recover. "She did something foolish and the flood took her. She wasn't the only victim but she was the only one from our missionary group."

"Until today," Adam reminded her.

"Yes. Until Rodrigo." The memory of the failed rescue would probably stick in her memory the rest of her life. As a nurse she had seen death, of course, but always in a hospital setting where she and her coworkers could work hard to stave off the inevitable. Acting as a volunteer EMT was harder. In the field she was reduced to guessing the severity of injuries and praying she was making the right diagnoses.

Losing Vicki had shaken Sara's faith to the point that she'd begun to question her effectiveness as a nurse *and* as a praying Christian. She'd sent up hours of fervent prayers for her cousin, yet Vicki was gone. If God had heard her and denied her request, as Scripture taught could happen, she wasn't at all happy about it, let alone ready to accept it.

And then there was the matter of poor Rodrigo. Why had he been inside the burning apartment? Why had he followed her home to Paradise? Vicki had seemed romantically attracted to him during their brief trip but they hadn't had time to develop a real relationship. Or had they?

Sara sighed quietly. Vicki was easy to like, easy to talk to. Men and women both warmed up to her immediately.

Unlike me. She chanced a sidelong glance at Adam. He'd been the same way, always laughing and enjoying her cousin's company a lot more than hers. The hardest test for Sara was when they had both bid him goodbye after his enlistment. Vicki had thrown her arms around his neck and even stolen a kiss, but when it had been Sara's turn Adam had acted embarrassed and resisted. All in all, she had loved her cousin and envied her at the same time.

Admitting that character flaw only added to Sara's sense of personal guilt. If Adam was right and her cousin had been purposely drowned, perhaps it was time to redeem herself by trying to uncover the truth.

But how? The only concrete tie to the missionary volunteers was Rodrigo. How was she ever going to learn how involved Vicki may have been with him? *Her diary!* Maybe she'd confided secrets in those pages. All Sara had to do was figure out a way to get a peek at the diary, assuming it had been sent home with her cousin's other personal possessions instead of accidentally destroyed or kept by the Texas police. It would be wonderful to uncover a budding romance because it might indicate that Rigo's visit to Paradise wasn't made for nefarious reasons.

Remembering Vicki's recent funeral and the way Helen, Vicki's mother, had wept and wailed and spread accusations of blame, Sara realized she'd almost rather be shot at again than have to approach that grieving woman and ask for a peek at Vicki's journal.

Another thought intruded, pulling her back to the elements that she *was* certain about. Her gaze met Adam's. "Wait a second. Rodrigo was inside the burning apartment. We know he couldn't have shot at us. So who did?"

Adam's incredulous expression made her feel foolish. When he huffed, rolled his eyes and said, "Took you long enough," she realized he had already asked himself the same question, probably hours ago.

As far as Sara was concerned, that proved how distracted she still was and how inept she'd been acting since returning to Paradise. For a person who prided herself on having it all together and functioning at the highest level, that realization was distressing. Not only was she more vulnerable while her brain took a vacation, so were the fire department volunteers she worked with. That failing was not acceptable to her and it certainly should not be acceptable to the fire chief.

What galled her most was that it was Adam Kane she cared most about impressing. Right now he was acting as if she should be able to focus, to think as clearly as she usually did.

Unfortunately, nothing could be further from the truth. Her life was falling apart around her and she hadn't a clue what to do about it.

THREE

Adam was determined to escort Sara home from the fire station that night whether she liked it or not. It wasn't a difficult chore since she lived in one of the apartments located above the offices and shops that lined all four sides of the Paradise town square. An old-fashioned courthouse sat in the center while police and fire stations were on Church Street, a short block east off the main drag.

"I jogged over. I can walk home," she insisted.

"Good for you. Humor me and get in." He held the door to his ranch pickup truck open for her before circling and sliding behind the wheel.

"Aren't you on duty tonight?"

"Yes. But I won't be far away. I have everything I need with me in case we get another call."

"I sure hope we don't."

"Yeah, me, too." He turned the final corner and pulled to the curb in front of Sara's apartment, above Cynthia Weatherly's insurance agency office. He got out and circled to open the passenger door.

"I can open my own doors, Adam."

"You're welcome," he said, clearly mocking.

"All right. Sorry. Thanks."

"My pleasure."

He trailed close behind, almost bumping into Sara when she stopped on the stairs and asked, "What are you doing?"

"Seeing you to your door."

"Why?"

"Because the chief of police asked me to." *And because there is no way I'm going to let you walk into possible danger without me.*

"That's ridiculous. Besides, since when is Chief Magill giving orders to Chief Ellis's firefighters?"

"Since one of his deputies has the flu and the others are still at the scene of the fire, looking for clues to who took those potshots at you."

Lights around the courthouse cast a yellowish glow and sent shadows all the way across the street to engulf the exterior staircase of the brick-faced building. It was situations like this that he'd learned to avoid in a war zone. Where there was darkness, there could be a hidden enemy—and often was.

Adam grasped Sara's upper arms through the sleeves of her light jacket. "Look, I don't care whether you believe you're in danger or not. Denial won't change reality. I don't know why you were a target tonight but I don't doubt for a second that you were. Whether or not the shooter meant to hit you is the only thing in question. He did miss."

She faced him, her chin jutting. "Are you this touchy because somebody tried to shoot you, too?"

The guttural noise Adam made as he threw both hands into the air was totally instinctive. The woman was impossible. And so special it made him crazy.

Refocusing, he managed to affect a calmer demeanor. "What is it with you, Sara? Why can't you just accept a good deed without psychoanalyzing it or inventing excuses for why it isn't genuine?"

He didn't know what kind of response he'd expected but it sure wasn't the one he got. Blinking back unshed tears, she stood tall. "Because I don't deserve it, Adam. You were right. It's my fault Vicki died. I should never have encouraged her to go on the mission trip with me in the first place, and I should have tied her to a tree that night if that was what it took to keep her safe."

"You had no way of knowing what was going to happen."

"No, but I did have strong misgivings. She was so excited and so proud to have uncovered what she thought was corruption I probably didn't try hard enough to talk her out of wading into the water. I could have stopped her, somehow. I should have done more." Sara paused to sniffle. "I should have gone with her, at the very least. Then maybe she'd still be alive."

Adam placed his hands gently on her shoulders and shook his head. "No, Sara. You could both have died."

"Maybe that would have been for the best."

As she covered her eyes and began to sob he gave in to the urge to embrace her, to pull her close. His heart was pounding and his breath shuddered as she wept against his uniform shirt.

He wanted to kiss her, to hold her and promise to never let her go. To assure her that losing her would have made his heart ache until the end of time.

Instead, he understood her survivor's guilt and simply said, "No. It wouldn't."

Sara didn't know how long they stood there. Nor did she care. These were the tears she hadn't yet been able to shed for her loss and having Adam there, supporting her, was an unbelievable relief and comfort. Finally, she eased away. "Sorry. I got your shirt all wet."

"It's not the first time I've been wet tonight," he quipped. Lifting his head he pointed with his chin. "Go on up whenever you're ready. I'll wait right here and watch until I see you're safely inside."

Managing a smile she wiped her damp cheeks with her fingertips. "I thought you were coming with me."

"I still will if that's what you want. I just thought it might be awkward, considering…"

This was his standard reaction to being too close to her, she recalled, feeling a little miffed. Well, she could hardly blame him. After all, she had just spent far too long clinging to him and crying her eyes out. Yes, her motives were innocent but it was perfectly natural for him to be uneasy. In view of the fluttering in her veins and an undeniable sense of excitement, she wasn't all that comfortable with their present situation, either.

Her smile widened and she patted his arm. "I get it. You're right. I would rather go up alone. I assure you, I'm quite capable of unlocking my own door. Been doing it for years. Good night, Adam."

"Good night."

Without further delay Sara completed her climb and fitted her key in the lock. Hesitating on the landing, she waved goodbye to him, hoping her crying jag hadn't permanently spoiled his good opinion of her. Adam had always been a reliable friend. A rock. Even if he never chose to see her as anything more than a buddy she'd have to be content.

Blanketed by her errant thoughts and feelings she broke eye contact.

Opened the door and took a step into the apartment.

Gasped. And screamed!

* * *

Adam was taking the stairs two at a time before he even realized he was moving. He burst in behind her, expecting a flesh-and-blood adversary. Instead, he was looking at the worst job of vandalism he'd ever seen. Furniture was slashed and overturned. Cupboards gaped open with their contents strewn on the floor, much of it broken. A fractured floor lamp lay across the end of the coffee table as if it had been used as a battering ram.

He pushed Sara behind him. "Stay here while I check the way I should have in the first place."

A crimson footprint low on one wall showed clearly because someone had dumped a gallon of red paint onto the hardwood floor and stepped in the puddle before kicking anything in the way. Paint was also flung up the walls and onto the sofa. What looked like the remains of all of Sara's clean nurse's scrubs had been stomped into the sticky mess until the fabric was hardly recognizable.

Circling the carnage as best he could, Adam checked the small bedroom and bath before returning to her.

"Anything else?" she asked with a tremor in her voice.

"Nobody's here but us, if that's what you mean," Adam assured her. "Call the police."

"I already did. They're pulling a couple of guys off the investigation of the shooting."

"Good. I don't expect them to find anything out there anyway. There's a better chance of turning up clues in here."

"Do you think the incidents are connected? I mean, the methods are very different."

"It's more likely than not. Whoever broke into your apartment must have figured you'd be gone with the volunteers and he'd have plenty of time to do this damage."

She wavered and he cupped her elbow to steady her. "You okay?"

"Not really. What am I going to do?"

"Take one thing at a time. Let's go back down to my truck to wait for the cops. You can't stay here." He could tell she was staggered by the avalanche of problems. "Look, why don't you call an out-of-town friend and see if she can put you up for a few nights? Leave Paradise until the cops have some answers."

"And chance bringing this kind of disaster on somebody else? No way. I suppose I can get a motel room. Or crash at the hospital in the employees' lounge."

"Neither of those choices is any safer for you than sleeping on one of the benches on the courthouse lawn across the street," Adam countered. A heartbeat later he added, "All right. You're coming to the ranch with me."

Sara rolled her eyes. "I don't think so."

"Why not?" He gave her his best skeptical look while wondering what she'd come up with for a plausible argument.

"Because it's not right."

"If it's okay with me and my brothers I don't see a problem. Besides, if you're uncomfortable being alone with me I can ask Carter and his wife to give you a place to sleep over at their house."

"No way. They have small children. I'd never take the chance they'd be put in danger."

Adam sobered. "So you *do* agree this is some kind of vendetta?"

"It must be," she answered softly. "I mean, look at my place. I won't be able to salvage any of my uniforms and the furniture is too spoiled to use again."

"That was yours, too?"

"Some of it was. Most came with the apartment. I

didn't need much room when my folks were still in Paradise, so I rented this place from Cynthia. Any time I started to get claustrophobic I could always drive to the farm and chill out in Dad's woods or fish in his pond. I suppose I should have looked for another place to live after they retired and moved to California, but I never got around to it."

"Your dad has a brother there, right?"

"Yes. And speaking of brothers, what are Carter and Kurt going to think when you show up on the ranch with a surprise houseguest?"

"I will be teased unmercifully until we tell them why you're there, but I'm willing to take the heat if you are. Mrs. K comes in a few days a week to cook and clean for me. I can ask her to stay over if it would make you more comfortable."

"We don't need to add another potential victim."

"Right." He had been smiling as he pictured being teased. Now, he sobered and sighed. "You really can trust me, you know."

"I know I can. It's not you—or your brothers—I'm worried about. It's town gossip. The Bible says we shouldn't do anything that gives even a hint of sin because it reflects poorly on our Lord."

"So, you're not avoiding me?"

Sara was shaking her head and Adam spotted fresh tears pooling in her eyes. "Of course not. We're old friends. I can't think of anyone I'd rather count on."

He was touched. "Thank you."

She swayed toward him for an instant and he imagined her falling into his embrace once again. Was that what he wanted? Was it fair to get involved with her, or with any woman, when he knew the fighting and killing he'd endured as a marine had hardened his heart and changed him in ways he was still discovering?

Getting down to basics, the most important thing was staying close to Sara until whoever was causing all the trouble was unmasked. How he was going to do that when they went to separate jobs was not going to be easy. Truth to tell, nothing about his relationship with Sara Southerland ever had been, even when they were kids and he had called her a little squirt.

Adam placed a hand at the small of her back and reached toward the door handle of his truck cab. "I think you'd better sit down before you fall down. Get in."

Her quick glance of consternation pleased him. Better she should be thinking about him than about her circumstances.

Braced with one hand on the door, one foot inside on the floorboard, Sara hesitated. "I hear sirens. Must be the police."

"Probably, since my pager hasn't gone off," he replied, feeling a sense of relief, short-lived though it might be. Paradise was always quiet at this time of night, so the curious would be peering out windows or trying to learn the reason for the sirens by listening to scanners and calling friends. Soon, they'd have plenty of company on the square and he'd have an even harder time keeping Sara isolated.

The wail of the patrol cars grew louder. Sara had remained standing, half in, half out of his pickup. Watching for the police, Adam noticed a white sedan cruising past followed by a dark-colored SUV. Both drivers were moving slowly and peering out at the area around the apartment.

Hair at the nape of his neck prickled. Few locals were

yet aware of the location of the break-in, so why were these drivers acting so interested?

Windows of both vehicles were rolled down, something he found a bit unusual considering the cool April night. Still, there was no law against getting fresh air.

Sara's drawn-out "Adam…" temporarily redirected his attention to her—only she wasn't looking at him, she was staring at the passing cars.

Suddenly her hands shot out. Her fingers fisted handfuls of his shirt like the talons of an eagle and yanked.

Adam tried to halt his fall but Sara had simultaneously thrown herself on to the truck seat, and momentum carried him down with her.

Then he felt the reverberation of multiple gunshots, heard a window shatter above his head and got the true picture.

Sara's quick thinking and decisive action had just saved his life. She might not know why thugs were pursuing her but in some ways she was behaving more rationally than he was. He couldn't believe he'd actually let her go alone to open that apartment door without backup.

Sounds of at least one engine revving echoed through the still night air. Tires squealed.

Adam pressed his cheek to Sara's and held her as tightly as he dared. Even a marine couldn't fight bullets with his bare hands. This was the last time he'd go anywhere unarmed until they were sure this threat had passed. Anybody who wanted to get to Sara Southerland would have to take him out first.

FOUR

Seconds crept by as if time had all but stopped. Sara made a token effort to wriggle free. Her back was bent against the edge of the seat and muscles were starting to cramp but, truth to tell, she was in no hurry to escape Adam's up-close-and-personal protection.

His voice was raspy. "You okay?"

"I—I think so. Are you?"

"Apparently."

She held very still as he levered himself onto his elbows and peered out at the street. "Are they gone?"

Nodding, Adam stood and held out his hand to her. Nothing pleased Sara more than the chance to grab it and hold on. His grip was firm and she could feel calluses from his hard work at both the fire station and his family-owned ranch. Yes, his touch was tender but there was also comforting substance and power to it.

Sara slid off the seat to stand beside him, keeping hold of his hand and helping Adam brush tiny glass crystals off his head and shoulders. "Did you see who it was?"

"Not clearly enough for an identification. How about you?" He ran a hand over his military haircut, then told Sara to bend forward so he could ruffle her hair, just in case there was glass in it, too.

She couldn't help shivering. "I hardly remember a thing. All I saw was the barrel of a gun pointing at us and I panicked. What a night." And judging by the sound of approaching sirens it wasn't over yet. "I didn't recognize anything about the cars. Did they have Missouri plates?"

"Don't know." Adam tried to let go of her hand. Sara resisted until he said, "I need to go talk to the sheriff. I'll be right over there."

"Then we both will be," she countered. "You're not getting rid of me that easily."

To her relief he looped an arm around her waist and pulled her to his side. "Never crossed my mind…"

She was ready to set aside her misgivings about the way Adam felt regarding their relationship until he added, "Buddy," instead of using her name.

Of course they were friends. That went without saying. And, if she were honest with herself, there was comfort in such camaraderie. Sara couldn't help it if her emotions had soared higher and faster than his. Or that no other man in her life had ever come close to measuring up to her childhood friend. Adam was not only handsome. He was kind and intelligent and could practically read her mind.

Except he was overlooking her when it came to romance, wasn't he? She sighed. There had been a time when she had thought his heart belonged to Vicki, yet he didn't seem to be grieving as much as Vicki's poor family. Then again, he'd been a marine and had seen combat so perhaps he was just good at hiding his feelings.

"I wish…" Sara muttered, surprised when Adam took notice.

"What?"

"I was talking to myself," she alibied, keeping her head bowed so he couldn't see her flaming cheeks.

He gave her a little squeeze. "Hang in there. As soon as the police let us go I'll get coverage for the last few hours of my shift and we'll go to my place."

Her wry wit surfaced and she gave him a lopsided smile. "You mean like a stray pup. It followed me home—can I keep it?"

"Yeah. Something like that." They joined a sheriff's deputy at his patrol car while other police officers were cautiously climbing the stairs to Sara's apartment, guns drawn.

Sara realized she had actually gone to school with this man, too, although she would never have predicted that such a troublesome kid would end up on the right side of the law. She nodded to him. "Hi, Tiger."

He stammered and cleared his throat. "You can call me Elmer. I don't use that nickname anymore."

"I thought you hated Elmer."

"I did. Still do. But my boss thought it sounded bad to go by Tiger, so I don't."

"Understandable."

Elmer eyed Adam. "Rough night, huh?"

"You have no idea. So far, Sara has been shot at three times, once here and twice at the scene of the fire we just put out over on County Road Seventeen."

"That's why they sent me this time. I heard there was a fatality out there."

Sara spoke up. "He died of smoke inhalation. Has the victim…has Rodrigo been sent to Springfield for an autopsy?"

"That's what we usually do, so I imagine so," Elmer replied. "Tell me about what happened here."

"It was a drive-by," Adam said. "We'd just discovered the vandalism in Sara's apartment and were waiting by my truck for the police."

"Did you recognize the vehicles involved?"

"No. One was an older car and one a fairly new, dark-colored SUV," Adam said while Sara nodded agreement.

"Maybe it was just teenagers stirring up trouble." As he spoke he was making a show of examining the truck with a flashlight. "Looks like the only damage was the busted window."

Despite her normally level temperament, Sara was beginning to get upset. "Listen, Tiger, you may have done that kind of thing when you were a kid but these shooters were not young. At least one of them wasn't. Part of his arm was sticking out the passenger-side window and I saw dark, splotchy colors on it, like maybe a tattoo, so don't pass this off as simple teenage mischief. My apartment is soaked in red paint, my furniture was slashed, and somebody has been taking potshots at me tonight. This is no little, inconsequential prank. Okay?"

"Got it. Sorry." Hands raised, he took a backward step toward his cruiser. "I'll radio what you told me and all units will keep a lookout, but with such generic descriptions of the vehicles I don't expect results. Come daylight we'll see if we can find what's left of the bullets that passed through your truck window. If you think of anything else, give dispatch a call."

Adam raised a hand in parting. "Will do. If you need us we'll be out at the ranch."

Sara noticed the officer's momentary pause before he entered his car. "I wish you hadn't told him that. It's going to be all over town by dawn, you know."

"Everything always is," Adam countered. "It's only when folks try to hide what they're doing that it becomes suspicious."

"I suppose you're right. At any rate, when they spot my car out at your ranch there will be no doubt."

"I said I'd drive you."

"I know. I just want my own wheels." Looking toward the diagonal parking spots across the street she frowned. "Hold on. Does my car look strange to you?"

He took a moment. "Yes. I'd say it has at least two flat tires."

"Terrific." Her shoulders sagged under the added burden. "I thought all they were aiming at was us and your truck. How could a stray bullet have hit more than one wheel?"

"We don't know that the shooting here has anything to do with your flats. Come on. As soon as we've reported the latest damage and I'm free to clean the glass off my truck seats, I'll check at the fire station and make sure there's enough coverage tonight." He looked at his watch. "It's only a couple of hours till my shift is over, anyway."

"Then how much time do you have off?" Sara asked, hoping it would be more than one day.

"Normally, we do three on and four off," Adam explained. "Under the circumstances I can probably take a little more time off than that."

"No. I don't want you to jeopardize your job. Besides, do you actually believe a few days will be long enough to solve these crimes?"

A shiver skittered up her spine when Adam looked straight into her eyes and said, "No. I'll be surprised if we ever figure everything out."

Sara was fighting tears when he added, "But I'll look out for you as long as you're in danger. I promise."

Adam already had firefighting gear with him in case of an emergency callback so he was able to arrange the scheduling change by phone.

He glanced over at Sara, seated beside him in the cab of his pickup. "It's all set. We can leave right away."

Although she didn't argue he could tell she was brooding. She proved it by saying, "I wish they'd let me back in my apartment to at least grab a change of clothes."

"You can borrow what you need from Carter's wife, Missy. I think she's about your size." Adam smiled, hoping to lift her mood. "I imagine the crime-scene folks will release your apartment in a day or so, but it will still be a mess."

"I probably should talk to my landlady in case the police don't call her right away. She's going to be very upset. I know I am."

"None of this is your fault, Sara."

Her head snapped around. "You're kidding, right? How can I not feel this is personal? Somebody is really mad at me and I haven't done one thing to earn it."

A few miles passed before Adam made a suggestion, hoping she wouldn't go ballistic on him. "Actually, I can think of a couple of possible reasons for your troubles. One, there's the matter of the thefts Vicki thought she had uncovered in Texas. Even if she was imagining a crime where there was none, she could have stirred the pot, so to speak."

"If there was no crime to be proved, then nobody from down south would care," Sara countered. "And there would be no good reason for Rodrigo to have come all the way up here unless he and Vicki had developed a serious romance."

"You assume he came because of her?"

"He must have. They were overly familiar on our trip and he ended up dying in her apartment. How much more connection do you want?"

"It's probably not going to be enough to satisfy the police about him but you do have a point."

"I certainly do." Adam felt her eyes on him and glanced her way just as she asked, "You said a couple of reasons. What's the second one?"

"Um. That's a bit harder to swallow. I was thinking of the Babcock family and their friends. Vicki's kin may be angrier than they acted at her funeral."

Sara was rolling her eyes as he returned his concentration to the road ahead. "If any of them are madder than my Aunt Helen, I'm in real trouble. If looks could have killed I'd already be on the wrong side of the grass."

"Helen was grieving, Sara. I'm sure she didn't mean whatever she said to you."

"That's the problem. There was no real confrontation. She just stared daggers at me." She sighed. "Maybe if my folks had managed to make it back for the service it wouldn't have been so bad, but Dad's heart condition won't permit travel."

Sara folded her arms and hugged herself. Adam thought he saw a shiver. "Are you cold? I never considered not being able to roll up the window."

"It's not the weather that chills me," she replied, "it's the atmosphere in this town since I came back without my cousin. Nobody seems to remember that she was my best friend. We were closer than sisters when we were growing up together."

Sober and sympathetic, Adam nodded. "I know. That's another reason for everybody to wonder why you weren't able to stop her the night she drowned."

"You, too, Adam?" Sara's words were shaky, her tone and inflection conveying disappointment.

He had overstepped, had hurt her when he'd merely been fishing for more information, for something, anything, that would put his and others' minds at rest. He reached across the seat to pat her shoulder and she shied away.

"Look, I'm not blaming you, Sara. I know how confusing emergencies can be and how things can go wrong no matter how careful and diligent we are. But I also know you're strong and will stand up for what you believe is right. Is that what happened? Did you let Vicki go because you wanted to nail the thieves as badly as she did? After all, stealing from a charity is the lowest kind of crime."

"Despicable." She shuddered. "But I wasn't thinking of that. All I really recall is that arguing with Vicki was like banging my head against a brick wall. She was every bit as stubborn as you think I am. If I had been the one determined to save that evidence I doubt she could have talked me out of it, either."

Adam refrained from agreeing and making things worse. He got it. He really did. But Sara seemed to be forgetting that her cousin had been his good friend, too, and he had also suffered a painful loss. Perhaps explaining that was how he could regain Sara's trust.

He cleared his throat, his hands fisting on the steering wheel, his jaw firm. This was hard to even consider, let alone express, but he'd do his best.

"I—I loved her, too, Sara. Losing Vicki may not have hurt me in exactly the same way but I do understand how you feel."

Watching out of the corner of his eye he saw her dabbing at her damp cheeks. Truth to tell, his own eyes were none too dry, although if she noticed he planned to blame the moisture on the aftereffects of fighting the fire.

"You loved her?"

"Of course I did. The three of us were great friends. That kind of special connection is rare."

"Yes. Yes, it is."

Adam noted that her head was lowered, her hair masking her cheeks, and her hands were folded in her lap. He wasn't sure if she was crying or praying or both. It hardly mattered. He'd shared personal insight that he'd revealed to no one else because he wanted Sara to see things from his perspective. To understand that she didn't have to grieve alone.

Remaining silent for the rest of the drive to his ranch, Adam let her mourn Vicki in her own way. He had shouted and railed at God when the news had reached Paradise and spread through the small town like wildfire. In the four days between that sad event and Sara's return he'd had time to regain his self-control, at least enough to hide his more turbulent emotions.

Now, weeks later, Sara knew the truth. Losing a friend for whatever reason was a terrible blow to a person's psyche as well as to his or her faith. His had been weak after his stint in the marine corps but recent events had tried it almost to the breaking point.

Adam thought of God and of the tasks he'd been given in his life. Hard ones. Painful ones. But, oh, so necessary. So right.

Yes, his faith had suffered and he continued to struggle against accepting the bad with the good. What he would have done, how he would have coped without a belief in a higher power, however, was unimaginable.

FIVE

Sara tensed as Adam wheeled his pickup beneath the wide, wrought-iron arch and onto the Kane ranch property. She had expected their arrival to be quiet if not stealthy. Instead, the main house was glowing from almost every window, including those upstairs.

"Oh, dear. It looks like they're up waiting for us."

"I called ahead," Adam said. "I didn't want to be shot as a prowler when I came in at an odd hour."

"Ah." She nodded. "That makes sense. I've lived in town for so long I'd forgotten how protective ranchers and farmers can be."

"Anybody out in the country needs to be proactive," he said. "We look after our own."

"Maybe that's what led you to becoming a firefighter."

"Maybe. I truly wanted to help people. What made you decided to volunteer as an EMT when it's so like your daily job?"

"Needed skills, I guess." That was all she intended to say. To have gone on about her reasons might have revealed too many personal truths besides altruism, such as wanting to be involved because it brought her closer to Adam in training meetings and, of course, when responding to emergency calls. The ones for medical aid required at least one regular engine or truck besides the rescue squad, so it was common for her to encounter him in the field.

"Well, we do need good volunteers and I'm glad you're one of them. You ought to try to recruit a few more medical professionals like yourself. We can always use more help."

"I'll remember that."

She shuddered as Adam parked. A gaggle of folks were waiting on the front porch. Farm dogs raced around his truck, jumping, barking and eager to see what all the excitement was about.

"Quite a welcoming committee," Sara said. "Kind of overwhelming, particularly since they know about the trouble in town." She paused and scowled. "You did warn them, didn't you?"

"Yes. I guess they're just glad to see you. What's the problem?"

"No problem." Sara forced a smile. "I'm so tired I was hoping to grab a quick shower and go to bed, not socialize."

"We won't keep you up. They just want to see that you're okay."

Was she okay? She sighed. Sure. She was fine considering that she could be in the hospital with a gunshot wound, or worse. Put that way she was more than fine. She was blessed beyond words. Nevertheless, running the gauntlet of Adam's big, magnanimous family was daunting.

She pasted a smile on her face, tried to control threatening tears and climbed out of the truck. This kind of warm welcome was unbelievable, particularly since half of Paradise seemed to blame her for Vicki's drowning. Or did they? This was not the first time it had occurred to Sara that she herself might feel so responsible she was imagining critical stares from others.

Helen Babcock's reaction had been a different story, of course. As Vicki's mother, Helen was entitled to place blame wherever she wanted. Sara was willing to tolerate the poor woman's hurtful accusations. Anything was okay if it helped her work through maternal grief and eventually cope with the horrendous loss. Yes, Helen had one remaining child—a grown son, Will—but that didn't negate Vicki's untimely death.

The Kanes gathered around Adam and Sara, peppering them with questions as he shepherded her up the porch steps. "We're fine, we're fine," he insisted. "Right now, what Sara needs most is a place to sleep and some clean clothes." His brother Carter's wife was holding a sleeping toddler while her husband held another. "Missy, can you loan her a few things until the police let Sara get back into her apartment?"

"Sure." The dark-haired, petite woman frowned. "I thought she was here because somebody shot at her. What happened to her apartment?"

Sara grimaced. "You wouldn't believe the mess. Somebody trashed the place and poured gallons of red paint all over everything."

Missy's brown eyes widened. "No way."

"Yes way," Adam said. "That's why she can't stay in town and why I thought it best to give her a break out here. Between me and Carter and Kurt we should be able to fend off any sneak attacks."

Sara noted how other members of Adam's family began to fall back, inching away from her. The parents carrying the sleepy children held them closer and actually covered the backs of their tousled heads with a hand.

"I really am sorry," Sara said. "I offered to get a motel

room or crash at the hospital but Adam insisted I come here." She glanced up at him. "Maybe this wasn't such a good idea after all."

"Nonsense." The group gave way as he ushered her through the front door. "You can have my room and I'll bunk with Kurt for a few nights. He snores but I have ear plugs."

The brother who looked enough like Adam to be his twin laughed. "Not as loud as you do, bro."

When Kurt grinned at Sara she was relieved. "I'm so tired tonight I can probably sleep through anything."

"Terrific. I'll run over to Missy and Carter's house and bring back some clothes for you." Kurt's smile gentled, making the resemblance to Adam even stronger.

"Thanks. I appreciate it."

"No sweat. Back in a few minutes."

Once they were alone, Adam gestured toward the stairway. "After you."

"Your brother is very nice. I didn't know him that well in school."

"That's right. You did skip a couple of grades, didn't you?"

She nodded. "Sadly, yes. My parents were so proud of my accomplishments they never considered the social repercussions of pushing me ahead of my peers. I never did fit in." *Except with you and Vicki.*

"Sure, you did."

Unwilling to argue the point, Sara dropped the subject. Adam had been a star high-school football player, successful 4-H and Future Farmers of America member, honor student and all-around popular jock, while she had struggled to maintain perfect grades to the exclusion of extracurricular activities.

He ushered her to a second-story room at the end of

a short hallway. "Here you go. I'll just grab a few of my things and get out of your way." He proceeded to do so, filling his arms. "You have your own private bath so nobody will bother you."

"Where will you be?" She knew her voice was not its normal pitch and hoped he didn't think she was whining.

"Right next door. Kurt was only half kidding. You'll probably hear one or both of us snoring."

That suited her just fine. She managed a smile. "Good."

Clutching the messy stack of clothes he backed through the open door. "Good night, then. I'll have Kurt drop the stuff from Missy right out here in the hall."

"Okay. Thanks."

And then he was gone, leaving Sara feeling as if she had just been marooned on a desert island while her ship sailed away. Only she wasn't truly alone, was she? Adam and his brother were going to be in the next room and if she could hear them snoring, they would also be able to hear her if she cried out.

Deciding to wait until she had something clean to put on after her shower, she looked around the room. It was clearly masculine and she imagined it might smell a little smoky because of its regular occupant. Though she and Adam were longtime friends she had never been in this room before. Truth to tell, she didn't remember much about the rest of the ranch, either, although she and Vicki had been invited out there to ride horses a few times.

Picturing Adam in his Western attire, complete with boots and a cowboy hat, made him seem entirely different. It was as if donning his fire department gear transformed him. He was very serious then, hardly ever laughing unless the training session or actual call was over. Once that happened, the firefighters behaved the same as overworked ER doctors and nurses and not only traded jokes, they rehashed recent traumas and looked for humor in everything. It was hard for civilians to understand doing that but Sara did. It was a necessary coping mechanism, one she imagined he had used as a marine on active duty, too.

She sighed as she strolled to the window and opened it to let in fresh air. A whippoorwill called in the distance and another, closer, answered. That meant they were nesting and chances of a late spring frost had passed.

The lights in the second house on the ranch flicked off, room after room. Missy and her family were going back to bed. Therefore, Kurt should have returned by now with her clean clothes.

She started to turn away from the window when something beyond the front gates caught her eye. Headlights of a car or truck were slowly passing on the road. Could they be looking for the Kane ranch? For her? Was that why the vehicle was creeping along?

Sara pushed back one side of the sheer curtains so she could see more clearly. The car was stopping. Her heart pounded erratically. The headlights blinked off.

Pivoting back against the wall she fought to catch her breath. She'd been silhouetted in that window like a paper practice target. Any hunter with a decent scope on his rifle would have no trouble sighting in on her. Getting her in his crosshairs. Pulling the trigger.

A scream lodged in her tight throat. She squelched the urge to wail and instead tried to call out.

"Adam?" *What a pitiful attempt*, she thought, disgusted with herself.

Taking a deeper breath she filled her lungs and did better. "Aa-dam! Adam!"

"Sara? Is that you?" was faint through the dividing wall but proved he'd heard her.

She redoubled her efforts with a hair-curling, spine-tingling, earsplitting version of "Adam!" that practically rattled the window pane.

He rushed through the bedroom door accompanied by his brother, half tripping over the pile of clothing from Missy.

"What is it?" His hands cupped her shoulders. "You're shaking."

"Outside. On the road..." she began.

While Adam continued to hold on to her, Kurt shaded his eyes and leaned closer to the window.

Sara jerked loose from Adam and launched herself at his brother, knocking him aside and ending up on the floor beside him. Hardly able to speak, she resorted to single words to try to make her point. "Car. Road. Target."

"You saw something from the window, you mean?" Adam asked, taking Kurt's place at the glass as if totally disregarding her warning.

"Get down!" It was a wail.

"Okay, okay." He gave his brother a hand up, then reached for Sara.

"Stay. Away. From. That. Window."

"We get it," Kurt said, dusting off his jeans as if he'd fallen in a muddy pasture instead of onto a rug. He crossed the room to flip off the ceiling light. "Now, we can see out but nobody can see in."

"The moon's full. They can still see the window even if they can't see inside," Adam reminded him.

"What makes you guys think anybody would be shooting at this house?" Kurt asked.

"Because they took out the side window in my truck a couple of hours ago, for starters," Adam explained.

"So you said. But that was back in town. I don't see a thing wrong here."

"Neither did Adam and I, earlier," Sara said, speaking past a telltale vocal tremor, "until the bullets started flying."

As far as Adam was concerned, anything that bothered Sara bothered him. Kurt was not quite so empathetic after they left her and went back to their shared bedroom.

"I'll take the shotgun and go have a look around," Adam said. "You can come along and back me up."

Kurt was shaking his head. "Not me, bro. I have better sense than to go prowling around in the dark—and so do you. Besides, neither of us saw any boogeymen."

"Sara thinks she did," Adam countered, keeping his voice down so she would overhear in the next room. "Something strange has been going on with her. I'm just not sure what it is yet."

"Well, she's pretty." Kurt grinned and winked. "Maybe you'd like to romance her and becoming her guard is your way to convince her to rely on you."

"Don't be ridiculous. We're just old friends and she needs help right now."

"Honestly?" The slightly younger brother's dark eyebrows arched. "Then I suppose you wouldn't mind if I asked her out."

"What?"

Kurt laughed. "You know what I mean. Boy. Girl. Dinner and a movie, maybe. A date?"

Adam knew exactly what his brother meant and he didn't like the idea one bit. Still, Sara could do worse. Kurt was a good man, a little immature sometimes but basically kind. And he had built-in financial stability via his inherited third of Kane Ranch. Given Adam's sense of responsibility for all the people in his life, he figured it wouldn't hurt to stand back and let his brother approach

Sara. She needed somebody stable. Someone she could count on in ways Adam wasn't convinced he could provide.

"Sure," he said with a forced smile. "Just bring me takeout when and if you go out to eat, and you have my blessing."

"Really? You're not just saying that?"

"No. I mean it." He sobered. "But if you break her heart you'll have me to reckon with, baby brother. Remember that and behave yourself."

Kurt backed away, hands raised, palms out, as Adam tucked the .12 gauge from their closet under one arm, grabbed his tan Stetson and headed for the door.

"Don't you have any camo?" his brother asked. "That big hat makes you stand out like a duck in a shooting gallery."

"Good point." He exchanged the familiar Stetson for a black baseball cap. "Better?"

"Yeah. Lots." Kurt laid a hand on his brother's shoulder to stop him. "Wait up. I will come with you."

"You don't have to."

The younger man chuckled. "Yes, I do."

"I appreciate it," Adam said. "That's what brothers are for, right?"

Kurt's laugh got louder and he clapped Adam on the back. "Sure. And if I go along to protect you, maybe some of that overblown hero worship Sara has for you will rub off on me."

"She doesn't think I'm a hero," Adam countered.

Kurt was still chuckling when they left the house together. Adam was not amused. He had never viewed himself as a hero. On the contrary, he was just a normal man doing his best. If the situations he encountered were tough, so be it. Life had never been easy for him the way it seemed to be for so many others. Perhaps that was because he took it too seriously. He couldn't help himself.

That's the way he judged his feelings in regard to Sara, too. The fondness he had for her was deep and solid, not frivolous the way his brother was treating it. There was nothing funny about caring for Sara while believing she would be far better off with someone other than himself.

Clenching his jaw and starting off the porch toward the barn to use it as temporary cover, Adam realized he'd have a much easier time accepting her choice of another man if that choice was anyone other than his handsome, easygoing brother.

SIX

From her upstairs vantage point, Sara watched the beams of two flashlights sweeping the yard. One was obviously Adam's and apparently Kurt had gone out with him. That was comforting.

Truth to tell, so was being there at the ranch with the Kane family. In the recent past she had always had Vicki as her closest confidant and partner in daily adventures and she missed her something awful.

Reminiscing, Sara remembered the mission trips she and Vicki had taken together, working hard passing out food and supplies or helping with cleanup. But neither of them had ever been asked to do office work. Vicki had reluctantly volunteered to take over the small task of keeping a running inventory when one of the regular Texas workers had become ill.

Everything would have been fine if her cousin hadn't had such a keen understanding of bookkeeping and spotted graft almost immediately. Finding cheats among all their devoted, honest peers had bothered Sara, too. It was Vicki, however, who had been convinced that they could unmask the cheaters themselves. Sara had adamantly disagreed, leading to an argument and Vicki's foolish actions the night she'd died.

Sara sighed and folded her arms to hug away the chill

of that memory. If their conversation hadn't gotten so heated, maybe Vicki would have been more willing to listen to reason. All they had to do was tell the police and leave it to them, Sara had said. Vicki had countered, insisting that without proof there would be no way to substantiate the thefts and the criminals would go on stealing from poor, traumatized victims. As things stood now, the only one who had paid any price was the dedicated young woman who had risked her life in the hopes she could single-handedly set things right.

In the yard below, Sara noted one of the small lights moving left. The other went right. The men were circling the house, obviously still searching for whoever had been in the vehicle that had stopped. In the dark, it was hard to see whether the car or truck had stayed there or driven off, and the harder Sara tried, the more distorted her vision became.

Shadows moved as if they had lives of their own. Fallen leaves were lifted from drifts and swirled past, giving substance to the rising wind. What moonlight there had been was now masked by clouds and the night seemed to be closing in around her.

Shivering and imagining all sorts of dangers, she wanted to race outside and call Adam back, drag him if necessary. Instead, she fisted her cell phone, scrolled to his number and pushed the call button.

One ring. Another. Finally, he answered. "What?"

"I—I just wanted to be sure you were okay. Have you found anything?"

"No."

"Why do you sound mad?"

"Because it's impossible to sneak up on anybody when a phone is flashing and playing a ring tone in your pocket."

"Sorry." And she was. She was also delighted to hear his voice, even angry. "Why don't you give it up and come back in the house?"

"May as well."

Sara stared at her phone. He'd hung up without even saying goodbye. That was not like him. Not a bit. Some of his bad mood was probably due to fatigue from fighting the fire and then experiencing the traumas that had followed, but that was no reason for him to act as though he blamed it all on her. Those distressing events might be important to Adam but they paled next to the loss of her dear cousin.

Suddenly, an intense wave of grief hit her like a tsunami. It rolled over her, crushing self-control and battering her breaking heart until she thought it would burst. Sara covered her mouth with both hands to try to mute the sobs while rivers of tears coursed down her cheeks.

She had wept very little and had felt numb a lot of the time since her return to Paradise. Now, without warning, she was so bereft she wanted to throw herself down and howl like an injured animal. Her mind kept calling out to God in mindless prayer. Her body trembled.

Then she heard rapid footsteps on the stairs. Adam was back. He already thought she was mentally unbalanced. He mustn't see her like this.

She bolted for the bathroom and slammed the door behind her, then grabbed a hand towel, held it tight to her face and shuddered with the effort of controlling herself.

Expecting him to go to his room with Kurt, she was astonished to hear his boots stamp through the bedroom and him call her name.

"Sara?" She wasn't ready to answer for fear he'd know she'd been upset and blame himself.

The door vibrated as Adam hit it with the flat of his hand and shouted, "Sara! Are you all right?"

"Y-yes."

"Then come help me. Kurt's been hurt."

Adam hardly glanced at her when she threw open the door. He'd spun on his heel and was already on his way.

She started after him. "What happened?"

"I'm not sure."

"Where is he?"

"I left him on the couch. He's talking but seems groggy. I called and called to you after I brought him in. Why didn't you come down?"

"I guess I didn't hear you with my door shut. Why didn't you phone?"

"Never thought of it," Adam admitted. And he hadn't. As a firefighter who was usually calm in crisis, he was disappointed in himself. Normally, he was able to compartmentalize his thoughts and actions but once in a while, like now, he reverted to instinct and simply acted.

"Okay. Give me room," Sara said, gently pushing him aside so she could lean over the injured man. "Kurt, can you hear me?"

"Mmm-hmm."

She held out an open hand. "Flashlight."

Adam slapped it into her palm the way a surgical nurse would deliver instruments to a doctor during an operation and watched as she peered into one of Kurt's eyes, then the other.

"Pupils are equal and reactive. Let's check his BP."

Adam unzipped his fire department emergency kit and handed her the stethoscope, then fitted the blood pressure cuff to Kurt's biceps and started to pump it up.

Sara was in place to take the readout before he reached full pressure.

"One forty over eighty," she said. "Not great but not too bad. His pulse is rapid but steady, respirations a little shallow." She looked up at Adam. "Was he ever unconscious?"

"I'm not sure. It was dark. When I found him he was getting up off the ground. Said he'd just tripped. I wanted you to look him over because I'm not sure I believe him."

Kurt opened one eye. "Hey, I'm right here, okay."

"Okay." Sara rocked back on her heels and looked up at Adam. "He's your brother, but if he were mine, I'd want him checked out in the ER."

Kurt opened the other eye. Adam saw him reaching for Sara's hand. "No ambulance."

Adam watched his brother's trademark smile begin as he gazed at the nurse. When Sara laid a hand on Kurt's forehead, the younger man closed his eyes and sighed. "That helps a lot."

She began to comb her fingers through his dark, wavy hair. "Let's look for a lump. You may still need expert medical care."

"Umm," Kurt murmured, "I'm getting it right now."

Adam was not impressed. "What'll it be? Ambulance or private vehicle?"

"No ambulance. No way," Kurt said, pushing himself up slowly and blinking as if clearing his head. "I just tripped. If I have to go get checked, I'll let you take me— as long as my favorite nurse comes along."

"Of course," Sara said.

"There's no need for you to go," Adam countered.

"Yes, there is. Your poor brother was hurt chasing the shadows I thought I saw and he deserves special attention."

Adam would have continued to argue if it hadn't occurred to him that there had to be a good reason why
Kurt had fallen so hard. If they could chalk his injury up
to deliberate head trauma instead of clumsiness, as he'd
claimed, then Sara would be safer sticking with them.

"I don't suppose you'd let me take two aspirin and call
you in the morning?" Kurt quipped.

"No aspirin until we're sure your head isn't badly injured," she replied.

Adam knew very well what she meant and it gave him
a shiver. If Kurt was bleeding internally, despite his ap-
parent lack of serious trauma, letting him take any meds
that thinned his blood would be bad.

Concern wiped away any trace of jealousy Adam had
felt and replaced it with brotherly love. Kurt was family and deserved his unwavering loyalty and attention.

That encompassing thought remained to vex him as
he and Sara guided his brother to the truck. Adam's mind
and heart already viewed all three of them as close. That
emotion included Sara, as it had for years, but he definitely wasn't seeing her as his sister. Oh, no. He was
regarding her as *his*. This was personal. And the more
time he spent with her, the stronger his unseen connection became.

Sara let Adam belt his brother into the front passenger
seat of his extended-cab pickup before climbing into the
second seat and taking her place directly behind Kurt.
She didn't think he was in any danger at the moment
and the hospital wasn't too far away so she hadn't insisted on waiting for an ambulance. Given their usual
response times, especially when the call wasn't critical,
she and Adam could have his brother delivered to ER

and being seen by a doctor before an ambulance would arrive at the ranch.

They passed through the arch and onto the dirt road. Habit made her look both ways for traffic despite the lack of headlights. Her breath caught. She gasped. Clamped a hand on Adam's shoulder. "Look!"

To their left, a large black vehicle was moving away. The country remained dark, yet there was no mistaking the boxy shape.

"I see it," Adam said as he wheeled in that direction to illuminate the rear of the fleeing SUV for a few moments. "License number?"

"No," she admitted sadly. "It's muddy. Unreadable."

Adam stopped and reversed.

"What are you doing?"

"Going to the ER."

"But…"

"No buts, Sara. We'd never catch them at night on these narrow roads without speeding recklessly and we can't further endanger my brother."

"It's okay with me if you want to chase him," Kurt said, but Sara could tell he was still not feeling as well as he should be.

Concern for her patient came first. So did the safety of her friends and in this instance those overlapped. "Okay. Hospital," she said. "At least you know I wasn't imagining things."

Kurt gingerly touched his scalp and winced. "I'd already decided to believe you."

Adam caught her eyes in the rearview mirror. "Yeah. Me, too."

There was no doubt in Adam's mind that the passengers in the darkened vehicle had been up to no good. If not for the recent attacks on Sara he might have assumed they were burglars or cattle rustlers scouting out the ranch for some future operation. They still might have been but he doubted it.

Every time he glanced in his mirrors to check for anyone tailing them he saw Sara. He couldn't help it. And the worry clouding her usually sunny expression tore at him. Finally, he decided it would be best to mention another possibility.

"That car with its lights out may have been cattle thieves."

"Oh, right," she drawled.

Kurt agreed with Adam. "Could be. Last week the Smiths took down a guy who was up to no good and held him until the sheriff got there." He chuckled softly. "Wish I'd seen it. I hear they made quite an impressive posse."

"Maybe we should recruit them to guard me, then," she quipped. "This is getting old fast."

"You never had any trouble before, did you?" Adam asked.

She shook her head and once again met his gaze in the mirror. "Not to speak of. There's always an unruly patient or two to consider but I don't recall any recent problems."

"I'd think your job would be pretty uneventful."

As he watched, Sara strained forward to lay her forearm across the back of the front seat and used it to support her chin. "Let me put it this way—a good day is when you don't have to call security or take time out to change your clothes in the middle of a shift. No nursing is as easy as people think. Patients are already feeling rotten when they get to us and it's downhill from there." She smiled slightly. "Except for folks like Miss Bessie. She's a sweetheart whether she's sick or well."

"Did you have a chance to talk to her at the fire scene?"

Adam asked. "She might have seen something next door before the fire started."

Sara was shaking her head. "No, but since we're heading for the hospital, maybe I'll have a chance to stop off in her room while we're there and have a chat."

What Adam wanted to do was insist she wait until he was free to accompany her. Common sense dictated he do so. Knowing what his old friend's reaction would probably be to a flat-out order, he refrained from issuing it. Sara was smart but stubborn. She'd been living on her own for long enough that she'd developed a greater sense of self, of marching to her own drummer, far beyond that which she had possessed as they were growing up.

Truth to tell, when he'd returned to Paradise after his military service he'd been astonished at her accomplishments as well as her confidence. Presently, however, he couldn't help wishing she were a bit more like her old self: the kind of person who relied on others and listened to friendly advice.

That irony struck him funny and he smiled, saw her face in the mirror and shook his head. This was no time for humor, yet professionals like them needed stress relief. Cracking jokes wasn't meant as disrespect. It was simply a way of helping them cope with the sorrow and disaster that was an integral part of their jobs.

Outsiders usually misunderstood, of course, which was why first responders and medical staff kept their wry humor to a minimum unless they were part of a private group, one that shared the sense of emotional need.

"Kurt will be fine," Adam said for mutual encouragement. "He has a hard head, just like the rest of our family."

His brother chuckled. "That's me."

Until Adam heard Kurt follow up the comment with a sound that reminded him of a cat's purr, he didn't realize Sara had laid a hand of comfort on the younger man's shoulder and was massaging it.

Kurt visibly relaxed. "Mmm, that feels good."

"Don't baby him too much," Adam warned her, "or he's likely to expect special treatment all the time."

"He deserves it," she countered. "He was hurt trying to help me stay safe."

"Hey, I was out there, too," Adam said, hoping he was infusing the comment with enough humor to cover his true feelings.

"Yes, but you weren't clobbered," Kurt reminded him.

"I thought you fell."

"Well, maybe," Kurt admitted. "But that's no reason for my pretty nurse to ignore my injury."

Adam rolled his eyes. "Oh, brother."

To his surprise, Sara reached over the seat and patted his shoulder, too. "You're both my heroes, okay? I don't require conks on the head as proof."

"Whew, that's good to hear," Adam quipped. The others were smiling along with him but behind his supposed good mood lurked a load of tension that he was loathe to acknowledge, even to himself. He had foolishly given Kurt his blessing to court Sara and was already dreading what might happen between them. Yes, his brother was a good man. And, yes, Sara deserved an upright husband to love and who would love her.

He simply did not want to let go or have to watch it happening.

SEVEN

Priority treatment in the small hospital's ER was facilitated by Sara's employment there. She didn't ask for anything special. It was simply provided as a matter of course.

Once Kurt and Adam were sequestered with the on-call doctor she quietly withdrew and entered the main hospital corridor. The first other nurse she encountered was able to tell her which room was Bessie Alt's.

Sara saw the open door. Lights were on over one of the beds so she entered to see for herself that Bessie was all right.

The sight of the elderly woman, bruised and receiving oxygen through a cannula, might have taken her aback if she had not been a professional. She smiled as their gazes met "Hi, Miss Bessie. How are you feeling?"

"Like I been whupped with an ugly stick," she replied. A chuckle was followed by a coughing spell. "Hoo-whee. That hurts."

"I know it must." Sara was checking the chart hanging at the end of the metal-framed bed. "Is there anything I can get for you while I'm here?"

"Yeah." She hacked again, then got temporary control. "The name of that dumb kid who burned down my place."

With a brief arch of her brows, Sara shook her head. "It won't help, I'm afraid. We think he was killed in the fire."

"No way," Bessie said.

"What?" The irate spark in the old woman's gaze made Sara scowl.

"I may be old and hard of hearing but the walls in that duplex were real thin. I heard a scuffle, then a shot. That was long before I smelled any smoke."

Tensing, Sara grabbed one of the bony hands and stared into Bessie's reddened, irritated eyes. "Are you positive it was a gunshot? Could it have been something else? Maybe a car backfiring or something?"

Bessie was adamant. "Nope. I was raised in the country, girl. I can tell you the difference between a pistol, a rifle or a scatter gun, just by the sounds they make. This was a pistol. And it was close by."

"Did you tell Sheriff Caruthers?"

"No, but Deputy Ott came by. I told him. Elmer never was the sharpest pencil in the box. I'm not real sure he took me seriously after he didn't catch any prowlers in my yard."

"I'll make sure the sheriff and town police hear about what you saw and heard, I promise." She leaned a little closer. "I was shot at, too, while the fire was burning, and the shooter got away."

"You take care, you hear. What was it? A pistol?"

"Sounded like a rifle to Adam Kane." Seeing a twinkle in the reddened eyes she added, "He was there with his crew to fight the fire."

The woman's leathery skin folded into the creases left from a lifetime of grinning. "Tsk, tsk, Sara. Why ain't you hooked and landed that big fella yet?"

"I haven't been fishing for him," she replied, carrying on the analogy.

"Maybe you don't think so but it's pretty plain he appreciates the bait you been usin'." Bessie eyed her tight jeans and formfitting shirt.

Embarrassed, Sara explained, "These are borrowed clothes. My apartment was trashed and I didn't have anything clean to wear so Missy Kane loaned me a few things."

"Be that as it may, don't underestimate yourself."

"Adam and I are just friends."

"It's better to start out that way," Bessie countered. "You know what you're gettin' and so does he."

"It isn't like that, Miss Bessie."

The elderly lady coughed into a tissue for a few seconds, then recovered and said, "Maybe it should be. You ever think of that?"

Sara wanted to argue but the words wouldn't come. It didn't matter whether or not Bessie was right. Adam had plainly said he'd been in love with Vicki. It wouldn't be right to wish for a change of heart on his part, at least not this soon.

Although it did seem as if he was beginning to show interest in her lately, Sara figured it had to be because he was grieving. It was normal for those who had lost a loved one to transfer their feelings to anyone who seemed to commiserate, to understand.

Is that what I'm doing, too? Sara asked herself. Adam was still here while Vicki was gone forever. And Sara missed her cousin as if she had been a beloved sister. Was she also seeing Adam as a lifeline thrown from a sinking ship? That was plausible. And so wrong of her. Surely they could uplift and support each other without beginning an ill-conceived romance.

She leaned down and air-kissed Miss Bessie's rosy cheek. "You rest now. I'll make sure the sheriff understands what you tried to tell Elmer. I don't think they realize you meant two men."

Bessie reached for Sara's hand and grasped it firmly. "You tell that Steve Caruthers that I still have all my marbles and he'd best listen. He wasn't good at paying attention when I taught him in the third grade, and it doesn't look like he's improved much."

Sara had to chuckle. "I'll tell him. And make him take you seriously." She paused to gather her thoughts. "What did the second person look like?"

"Young. They both was. One was a kinda little guy and the other one was heftier. Enough alike that they coulda been brothers, I guess. Same dark hair and olive complexion. The short one took after that handsome actor—can't think of his name. I'd 'ave figured he'd come courtin' Vicki if she hadn't gone to glory."

"I think Rigo did have eyes for her when we were down in Texas. I just can't figure out what brought him to Paradise."

Nodding pensively, Bessie sighed. "Let's pray he made it to the real place, up yonder."

All Sara said was, "Amen."

Left to his own devices while a technician wheeled Kurt to radiology, Adam paced the hallway. He'd expected Sara to linger nearby but when he'd looked for her, she was gone. He knew she was comfortable in the hospital atmosphere and he shouldn't worry. He also knew she was too innately adventurous. There was no telling what she might get up to without his well-grounded influence.

That thought grated. How in the world was he going to keep her safe when she ventured off on her own the minute he was otherwise occupied? Such as now. Chances were she was still on hospital grounds, most likely inside the building, yet he had no idea if she'd located Bessie, where she might be or if she was still looking.

Adam had checked in with the county sheriff, watched a smiling Kurt return from X-ray and was presently leaning against a wall, watching for Sara and feigning nonchalance. He'd intended to berate her but the moment he spotted her coming toward him he was so relieved all negative thoughts fled.

Straightening, he smiled. "Glad you're back. I was about to send out a posse."

"I went to see if Miss Bessie was awake. She was."

"How is she doing?"

"As well as can be expected for someone with breathing difficulties who got her lungs full of smoke."

Adam opened the interior door to the ER and held it for her. "After you."

"How's Kurt?"

"Fine. Ornery. Typical."

"Good to hear. The rest of your family would probably kick me out if he'd been badly injured."

"Never." Adam placed his hand lightly at the back of her waist and guided her to where his brother was now perched on the edge of a cot. It didn't surprise him to see Sara check the dressing before picking up the doctor's orders and reading them. "Looks good, Kurt. You're signed out. Ready to go?"

"Boy, am I. This place smells funny."

She laughed softly. "I never notice. Guess I'm used to it."

"Yeah—" the younger brother gave her a lopsided grin "—like the fragrance of the horse barn out at the ranch. I actually kind of like that."

"To each his own," Adam said, positioning himself on the opposite side, ready to assist. "Can you walk?"

"'Course I can. Oops!"

"If he was carrying on too much they may have given him a light sedative while they were working on his scalp," Sara explained. "It wouldn't have been strong since he had a head injury. They wouldn't want to mask symptoms."

"I *told* everybody I was fine," Kurt grumbled before recovering and directing a warm smile at Sara.

Seeing her smiling back and sensing the unspoken camaraderie between his brother and his childhood friend hit Adam hard. Too hard. He clenched his jaw. What was the matter with him? Sara wasn't his woman; not in the way his heart kept insisting. She had every right to be interested in Kurt or any other single guy. Yes, it bothered him. And, yes, he felt like a fool when jealousy edged into his mind. But that didn't change what was right and true.

The smartest course for him, Adam reasoned, was to redirect their focus by changing the subject. "So, what did you learn from Miss Bessie?" he asked Sara.

"A lot." Her smile faded. "She's sure there were two men at the duplex before it caught fire. The description of one of them matches Rodrigo. The other one I'm not so sure about."

"Who do you think it was?"

"Could be almost anybody from the mission trip. We had volunteers from all over Texas as well as Arkansas and Missouri. Bessie said the other guy was also young but bigger, heavier. She also said she called the sheriff to report prowlers but by the time Elmer showed up he thought the guys had left."

"Apparently not."

"Not if they're the ones who started the fire."

Pausing to unlock his truck doors, Adam scowled over at her. "You have doubts?"

"Sure. Why not? Being strangers in town doesn't automatically make them criminals."

"True. But one was found inside the burning building."

"There is that."

Adam waited until they were all back in the truck before he continued questioning her. "How well did you know the fire victim?"

"Not very well. Vicki got along with everybody but I didn't really form any lasting friendships while we were down there. Until Miss Bessie told me there was at least one other man with Rigo, I had assumed he'd come to pay his respects to Vicki's family."

"Maybe he did."

"And just happened to end up shot in her apartment?"

Adam's pulse jumped. "Shot? Who told you he was shot?"

"Bessie. She's sure she heard the sound."

Did he dare tell her what he'd learned mere minutes before? Why not? She'd hear the details soon enough. He caught her gaze in the mirror once again. "She was right. We won't have the full story until the medical examiner up in Springfield does the autopsy, but paramedics found a wound in his lower back. They think a bullet hit his liver or a kidney, so he bled out in minutes."

"Smoke inhalation didn't kill him?"

"Apparently not. He'd have had to still be breathing to make that happen."

Beside Adam in the front seat, Kurt snorted. "I can't believe you two. Somebody died and you're talking about him as casually as you'd discuss the weather. What gives with that, anyway?"

Sara patted his shoulder from behind again. "It goes with our jobs, I guess. If we let ourselves get too emotional about the people we come in contact with, it can adversely affect our performance, our necessary efficiency." She sighed. "It is harder when you're treating friends, though. That's one of the drawbacks of working in a small community like Paradise." She glanced to her left. "Right, Adam?"

"Right. And when you lose somebody you hurt doubly, once for the personal loss and again for the failure to save their life."

"Yes," Sara agreed quietly, "whether you were present to render aid or not."

Kurt huffed. "That's nuts."

"Nevertheless, it's true for most of us," Sara said.

"So that's why you and Adam are both acting so strange about your cousin Vicki? I still don't get it. He was here so he had no chance to prevent her death. And you were stranded by the flood water the same as everybody else. How in the world could either of you be responsible?"

Adam waited for Sara to speak. When she didn't, he tried to explain his own pain. "I didn't claim it made sense, okay? It's as if you saw a tornado headed for the ranch and knew you were likely to lose cattle but were powerless to stop it. You'd do what you could, of course, and I did in regard to Vicki when I advised her to stay in Paradise. Beyond that, I guess I just hate the idea that she wouldn't take my advice."

Behind him, Sara sniffled before she said, "It was my idea to join the mission-group relief efforts and Vicki wanted to go along, so I arranged it. When you consider Adam's opinion, that makes me totally at fault. I took her. I tried to keep her safe. And I failed."

"Hey, I never meant that," Adam argued. If they hadn't been nearly to the ranch he'd have pulled over and... *And what? Taken her in my arms? Held her and assured her*

I knew she'd done her best, as she always did? Perhaps if Kurt hadn't been with them he would have, but since there were three in the truck he decided to keep going.

He did, however, try to reason with her. "Look, Sara. You may have encouraged her to go with you but it was Vicki's decision to try to get back to the office trailer to grab those receipts. She made up her own mind."

"What receipts?" Kurt asked. "What's going on here? Are you two involved with something more than a stalker?"

Although Adam nodded, his explanation purposely lacked substance. "We don't really know what's going on. The guy who died in the fire was from Texas and Miss Bessie says he had company. That's pretty much all we know so far."

"You think the guys in the truck out at the ranch were from Texas, too?"

Sara answered, "It's highly possible." She sniffled again. "Vicki thought she had uncovered theft in the mission's books and was planning to expose whoever was responsible. Once she got her teeth into a just cause she hung on like a bulldogger bringing down a steer."

The younger man was nodding. "Now *that* I can relate to. Give me an exciting rodeo any day over working in a hospital or fire station."

"To each his own," Adam said flatly. "There can be plenty of excitement other places."

For him, the conundrum lay not in his job but in wishing for something or someone beyond the realm of possibilities. He knew all about the wisdom of keeping a narrow focus after having been in the military, and it was just as important to do so in civilian life. Marines had strict rules of engagement and protocol. Adam's current circumstances lacked such cut-and-dried restrictions and therefore left him wondering what was best, right and logical.

How could he possibly decide that when he didn't even know what he really wanted or whether it was fair to pursue it? *Her.*

Another glance back at Sara's reflection showed him that she had scooted over, rested her chin on her folded arms across the back corner of his seat and closed her eyes. A wisp of her hair had drifted across her forehead. If he had been facing her he would have been tempted to brush it back with his fingertips.

His imagination did just that and he shivered without actually touching her.

To his right, Adam saw his brother's head cant and his eyebrows arch. Kurt had been watching him, had apparently noticed his telling reaction to Sara's reflection and was now staring quizzically.

Rather than engage in conversation, particularly about the pretty nurse, Adam gripped the wheel more tightly, faced forward and kept driving as if he hadn't seen his brother's reaction. It wasn't a perfect response but it would do. For now.

EIGHT

Sara was positive she wouldn't sleep a wink after they got home from their adventures that night. She was wrong. It was the aroma of coffee brewing and bacon frying that woke her the next morning. By the time she dressed and came down to the kitchen, Adam had gone outside to do chores.

His brother remained. "Hello, sleepyhead."

"Good morning, Kurt. Speaking of heads, how is yours feeling?"

He made a silly face and patted the tiny bandage. "I may need private nursing care so it's a good thing you're here."

She laughed. "You are so full of it!"

"That's what everybody says." Kurt was laughing with her. "Just trying to live up to the image."

"Well, you're doing a good job." She peered past him. "Is there any bacon left?"

"Sure is. We ate all the leftover coffee cake Mrs. K made the last time she was here but I've got farm-fresh eggs, if you want. Grab a cup of coffee and I'll fry you some."

Sara was already on her way to the steaming pot where a clean mug awaited her. "One egg is fine. Over easy, please."

He bowed with a theatrical flourish. "My pleasure. Toast?"

"I can make that."

"Pop another slice in for me, too, will you?"

"Gotcha." As Sara waited for the toast to brown she thought about the easy camaraderie they were enjoying. Why couldn't she and Adam share pleasurable times like this anymore? They used to. So what was different? What had changed? Was it her? Him?

Both was the likely answer. She had gotten her nursing degree while he'd been off fighting a war. They had each matured, had developed a stronger sense of self, of their places in life. By itself that was not a bad thing. In their case, however, it had seemed to cause changes that she failed to fully understand. And until she did, there was little chance she could figure out how to return to the easy friendship they had once shared.

Sipping her coffee, she gazed out the kitchen window and spotted Adam. He was dressed for ranch work in boots, jeans, denim jacket and Western hat and had paused by a corral to stroke the nose of a tall roan horse.

Both Sara's hands gripped the mug to steady herself while her heart leaped into an adrenaline high. The sight of him was dear as well as painful. He had rescued her, literally, and provided refuge, yet he was acting as if doing so was nothing more than an extension of his fire department job. Which it undoubtedly was.

She sighed, put down her coffee and buttered the hot toast. Kurt had prepared her a plate and was carrying it to the round oak table at one end of the kitchen, so she followed.

"Did Adam eat already?"

"Oh, yeah. Hours ago. He got antsy so I waited for you, instead."

"Thanks. That was thoughtful."

"Yeah, well, I imagine he'll be on my case the rest of the day for making him do morning chores alone."

"Sorry. You didn't need to hang around and wait for me, you know. I could have muddled through breakfast by myself."

Kurt's smile was broad, his eyes twinkling. "That's not what Adam said. He says you need your own Mrs. K. because your home-cooking is survivalist. If it doesn't look like it might kill you, you eat it."

Sara rolled her eyes. "Flattering."

"True?"

"Maybe." She had to smile at Kurt's impish expression. "What else did Adam say about me?"

The reddening of his cheeks was evident despite the dusky shadow that proved he needed a shave. Sara put down her fork and scowled at him. "What?"

Kurt cleared his throat and gave her a sheepish look. "You mean other than telling me he wouldn't be mad if I asked you out?"

It was several seconds before she realized her jaw had dropped. She snapped it shut. "What?"

"It was just a courtesy on my part, okay? I didn't want him to think I was poaching in his territory."

"His *territory*?" Shock was being replaced with comprehension followed quickly by righteous anger. "So, let me get this straight. You asked Adam for permission to date me as if he were my official guardian and he graciously gave my rights away?"

"Um, yeah, only it wasn't exactly like that."

No longer hungry, Sara pushed away from the table and stood, hands on her hips. There was one sure way to find out what had been meant as well as what had been said. She was going to find Adam and ask him to his face.

If his story matched that of his brother, she intended to inform him that although she did appreciate his offer of a temporary place to stay, she had not ceded her individuality or anything else to him—or to his family.

It was bad enough that an unknown person or persons were making her life miserable. She didn't need more consternation from her friends.

Adam had tied a bay mare's lead rope to a hitching ring by the stable and was currying her glossy coat when he looked up and saw Sara approaching. A smile began to lift the corners of his mouth, then stopped. Judging by her stiff walk and serious expression, either something else had gone bad or she'd gotten up on the wrong side of the bed.

He straightened, running a palm over the horse's flank to steady her and telegraph his movement. A nod to Sara followed. "Morning."

"Morning." She kept coming until she was within nibbling distance of the mischievous mare, then stepped back slightly to keep clear of her velvety-soft upper lip.

"Did you find the coffee and something to eat?"

"Yes. Your brother waited for me to come downstairs."

"Good." Adam stared, waiting, frowning. "Who put the burr under your saddle? Did Kurt get out of line? If he did, I'll—"

"You'll what? You gave him permission to make a pass at me, didn't you?"

Adam was dumbfounded. "I what?"

"You heard me. He says you told him it was okay to date me." Her fisted hands returned to her hips. "Don't *I* get a say?"

"Don't be ridiculous. Of course you do."

"Then what in the world made you grant him rights

that weren't yours to give? I feel like a puppy that was abandoned by the wayside because nobody wanted it."

He raised a hand, almost touched her arm, then withdrew. Sara was angry and looking for explanations, not asking for physical comfort. They both needed answers, the least of which involved their personal relationship. However, unless and until they figured out who had been stalking and attacking her, they needed to stay focused on possible dangers, not be distracted by emotion.

Standing tall, Adam blew a sigh. This was a proud, intelligent woman who deserved better than she'd been getting since returning to Paradise. If she pulled away from him, from his protection, because of a misunderstanding, the fault would lie with him. Only the truth would do—at least part of it.

"Look," he said, forcing a slight smile in the hopes it would soften his words, "it's like this. Kurt and I were strong rivals when we were kids, and he didn't want to step on my toes in case I thought of you as my girlfriend."

"Terrific. Go on."

"It's simple, really. When he asked if I'd mind if he tried to date you, I told him it was okay with me. I wasn't giving you away. We'll always be good friends. But that doesn't mean you can't have a life beyond our special friendship. Am I right?"

Observing her closely he wanted to be certain she understood before he dropped the subject. The relief he had expected to see looked more like sadness. When she finally nodded and said, "Yes," her lower lip was trembling.

She turned away. Adam reached for her. The impatient horse nudged him with her nose and pushed his arm to the side.

The jealous mare was right. Going after Sara would do nothing but complicate matters, but he did intend to have a talk with his outspoken brother. The less angst there was among the three of them, the easier it was going to be to keep Sara safe.

Speaking of which… Adam pulled out his cell phone and dialed the sheriff. Ballistics results on the various bullets would take a while since that information would come from Springfield or Jefferson City. Any finger-prints found in Sara's vandalized apartment should have a quicker match, assuming they were in the national crimi-nal database, AFIS.

And if they weren't? He breathed deeply and released another sigh. If the prints had no match they'd be right back where they'd started. Sara would still be someone's target.

She wanted to cry. She also wanted to pitch a scream-ing rant. Neither choice seemed sensible, so she merely returned to her temporary bedroom to think while she bat-tled the tears that kept gathering behind her lashes every time she thought of what Adam had said. He'd meant well. She knew that. There was no reason for her to be upset by hearing the truth. Yet she was hurt. Deeply.

"It's not his fault he can't see me as more than his childhood buddy," she told herself. "That's a hard mold to break."

Besides, if she ever did convince him to view her as a grown, appealing woman, it might spoil the dearest friendship she'd ever had with any man. That was the crux of the problem, wasn't it? Adam was all man, with the honor of a brave marine, the attraction of his job as a fire-fighter and the ruggedness of a working cowboy. Look-ing at him was akin to seeing all those impressive figures rolled into one, making him very hard to resist. Not that she'd had any trouble fending off his advances. On the contrary, his standoffishness was driving her crazy.

Images of throwing herself at him popped into her head and made her blush. That would be so wrong. And so much fun, assuming he didn't push her away and give her another lecture about being sensible. Maybe she didn't want to be so sensible. Maybe she wanted to take her chances and find out if there was any tiny spark between them before she so much as considered dating anyone else, particularly Kurt.

The biggest problem with doing that, as far as Sara was concerned, was the possibility of being thrust into close proximity with Adam in the future. His was a close family. No way was she going to allow herself to become a part of the Kane clan via marriage unless it was to Adam. Anything else would be too painful, especially if and when he found himself a bride.

Images of herself in a bridal gown, standing at the rear of the church sanctuary and looking toward the altar, immediately filled her mind. A tall, handsome groom awaited her. She couldn't make out his face but her heart was clear about it. If the stalwart man in a Western-cut suit wasn't Adam Kane, she was not marching down that aisle. Period.

The arrival of the sheriff himself brought Adam out of the barn and back to the ranch house at a jog. "Morning, Steve. Anything new on the Southerland case?"

"Depends." He scanned the yard. "Where is she?"

"Inside as far as I know. Sara's not in the best mood today."

"Yeah, I imagine she isn't." Hooking his thumbs into his equipment belt he hitched it up before leaning against his patrol car. "We figured out what kind of boot made those prints in the red paint. Not that it helps much. It was a size eleven with a walking heel."

"Cowboy boot, you mean?"

"Sure looks it. Well worn. The toe was curled up just enough to keep from touching the wall when the wearer kicked it, but the experts still say it had a more pointed toe than your normal shoe."

"Great." Adam raked his hands over his short haircut in frustration. "That eliminates nobody."

Steve was shaking his head. "It helps a tad. We know it wasn't a woman unless she had really big feet. It also wasn't one of those fellas who like hiking boots or trainers with waffled soles." He paused, canted his head to the side and added, "Like the victim your boys pulled out of the fire. His rubber soles melted."

"I see. So you're thinking whoever was with him was probably wearing the same kind of shoes."

"I am. Doesn't matter where they were from. Not every Texan dresses like a cowboy, you know." He chuckled, making his belt jiggle. "We got more Stetsons and spurs around these parts than half of Texas."

Adam agreed. "Okay, so now what? Do we start looking for worn-out boots with red paint on them?"

"If our vandal is dumber than dirt, we do. I gathered he ain't, judging by the complete mess he made of Sara's apartment. Which reminds me. I heard from Miz Weatherly. She's still waitin' on her insurance man to come look at the damage but she's found Sara a new place right around the corner, a little house that sits behind the electric co-op."

"No way. She's staying right here until we figure out who's been causing all the trouble."

"'We'?" The chubby lawman laughed raucously. "Where'd you get your badge, son? In a cereal box?"

"You know what I mean. She's better off away from town."

From behind him he heard a feminine voice say, "Suppose you let me be the judge of that."

Adam wheeled and confronted her. Saw sparks of anger flashing in her gaze. "I thought you were in the house."

"Obviously." Smiling at the sheriff she approached. "Did I hear correctly? You have a place for me to stay while my old apartment is being redone?"

"Miz Cynthia does," Steve replied. "That's one of the reasons I stopped by. I wanted to tell you in person and see what you decided to do."

"I'm going back to Paradise, of course," Sara said, shooting a look at Adam that dared him to argue. "Is the new place ready now?"

"There's a full crew sprucin' it up for you this morning. You should be able to move in right quick."

"Good. It's not like I have a lot of personal stuff that wasn't ruined by that paint."

Adam just stared. She already thought he was trying to run her life but, truth to tell, somebody with good sense had better take charge because Sara wasn't thinking clearly. "You'll be a lot safer out here with us," he said.

"And farther from work. And dependent upon the kindness of your family when I'm fully capable of taking care of myself," she countered. She turned to the sheriff. "Do you suppose I could hitch a ride back to town with you? My flat tires should have been fixed by now and I don't like being stranded without wheels." She gave a nervous-sounding chuckle. "I can't see myself saddling up and riding a horse to work."

"I'd buy a ticket to see that," the sheriff joked.

It only took Adam an instant after saying, "All right.

I'll take you," for him to realize she wasn't going to allow it. A hardening of her expression left no doubt. Neither did her reply.

"I prefer to ride with Sheriff Caruthers if it won't take him out of his way. Otherwise, perhaps he can send Deputy Ott back for me."

"It'd be my pleasure, ma'am," the older man said. "Why don't you go pack? I'll wait right here for you."

"Thank you, Sheriff."

Adam held his tongue until Sara slammed the back door behind her. "You could have told her you were busy."

"Why? So you can get yourself into more of a pickle? She's dynamite, son. The more information I get back, the worse this whole thing sounds."

"Explain."

"For starters, that fella that got himself shot was a member of a gang. Been arrested before and spent several months in juvie. I only know that because I got a buddy workin' down near the border with Mexico."

"That doesn't mean Sara is involved."

"'Course not. But there is a fair chance the dead guy's buddy is connected, too. And if he's still around he can be dangerous. Plus, there may be more than the two strangers Miz Bessie saw."

"All the more reason why Sara should stay out here."

"I gotta disagree. You're too far from town if something does go down. And this is a big county. I can't assign any of my deputies to patrol out here on a regular basis. If she's in town, the police department can keep an eye on her a lot easier."

"I don't like this," Adam said flatly.

The sheriff snorted a chuckle. "We finally agree on something." He gestured toward the ranch house. "If I were you, I'd go tell her goodbye and then stand back so you don't get run over when she heads for the door. I got the feelin' she's gonna mow down any resistance, including you."

"*Especially* me," Adam said cynically. "She was upset before you ever showed up. If I did anything to try to stop her at this point she'd throw a fit."

"So, no sweat. We let her have her way and work around her."

"It's not that simple," Adam argued.

Steve chuckled again. "Son, she's a woman. Nothing about them is ever simple, 'specially when a fella's heart is involved."

"Meaning *mine*? No way."

That claim set off the sheriff as if Adam had just delivered the punch line to a hilarious joke. Shaking his head and laughing, Steve arched his eyebrows. "You may be able to lie to yourself, but you'll never convince the rest of Paradise that you and Miz Sara aren't an item. All a body has to do is see your faces when you look at each other to tell."

Adam set his jaw, his lips pressed tightly together, before answering, "I've never gotten that impression from her and I've known her most of her life."

"Maybe that's the problem. You know her too well."

Could it be that simple? Was he seeing what he expected to see rather than studying her face as he would that of a woman with whom he was not so familiar? Adam rejected the idea. He knew Sara almost as well as he knew himself and she'd never shown romantic leanings toward him. He, on the other hand…

Warmth crept up Adam's neck and infused his cheeks with more color. If Steve had noticed his undue interest in her then perhaps others had, too—although Kurt seemed oblivious, so it couldn't be that evident. Besides, all he'd have to do is explain that he was concerned for her safety, which he was, and that would defuse most rumors.

He looked toward the kitchen door as it opened. Sara was toting a pillowcase that apparently contained Missy's clothing. What she was going to do about scrubs when she needed to return to work was another unanswered question.

Instead of approaching closely she called, "Thanks for everything, Adam," then went directly to the passenger side of the patrol car and climbed in as soon as the sheriff released the automatic locks.

Adam knew it was likely to anger her but he was going to follow them all the way to town. He simply had to. She might be as thorny as wild Ozark blackberry vines but he didn't care. He'd be there for her whether she liked it or not.

NINE

Sara felt terrible about the way she'd treated Adam, and the farther away from the ranch she and the sheriff traveled, the worse her guilt became. What was it about Adam that got under her skin so badly? In retrospect, he hadn't really done anything so terrible. She was just used to calling the shots, to organizing her own life and making decisions without anyone's help. That was as normal and necessary as breathing. She wasn't wrong to be self-determined. But she knew she should have expressed her independence with a little more kindness and understanding, particularly to an old friend.

Adam Kane had tried to boss her around since they were children. Back then she had let him get away with it, for the most part. This situation was different, although she had yet to fully understand what had changed their relationship and when. All Sara knew was that being around him had begun to make her anxious lately, as if she were teetering on the edge of a steep cliff and in danger of toppling over. Of course, that was ridiculous. Yet the more she thought about Adam, the more contrite she grew.

The sheriff hadn't commented much during the short drive and as he pulled up to the garage where her car was having the damaged tires replaced, Sara broke the silence. "Thanks for the lift. I guess I owe Adam an apology, huh?"

"Maybe." The older man smiled. "I don't know what made you so all-fired mad but the poor guy's motives were probably good."

"I know. And I snapped his head off." She gathered the open end of the pillowcase in one hand and started to get out of the car. "When you see Adam, will you tell him I'm sorry?"

Steve's smile widened into a grin and he tilted his cap back by its brim. "Won't need to." Swiveling slightly, he gestured over his shoulder at the truck parking behind them. "You can tell him yourself."

Sara almost lost her grip on the pillowcase. She was delighted to see Adam, yet upset that he had trailed her to town. What in the world was wrong with her? If she hadn't known better she'd have suspected that she had taken the blow to the head instead of Kurt. Obviously, something had happened to damage her usually predictable brain because it certainly wasn't lining up known facts the sensible way it had in the past.

As soon as she closed the passenger door of the patrol car the sheriff pulled away, leaving her standing there alone. She watched Adam climb out of his truck, put on his Stetson and stride toward her. His unreadable expression left her with no clues as to his mood. That didn't matter. She knew what she must do and say.

Raising her free hand, palm out like a traffic cop, she said, "Stop. Before you say a word, let me tell you how sorry I am. I should never have snapped at you the way I did. I know you meant well."

Shock replaced the hard set of his jaw and glint in his

eyes. His pace slowed and he eased up to her. "I want nothing but the best for you, Sara."

"I know. Still friends?" She held out her hand, wondering why it was taking him so long to shake it.

Adam stuffed his hands into his pockets instead. "Sure. Friends."

"Good. I'm going to bail out my car, then go talk to Cynthia about my new place. Want to come with me?"

"Nope. You'll do fine by yourself. I'll just pop over to the fire station and see if anybody has located the origin of the fire at Vicki's."

She was taken aback. "Okay. See you."

"Yeah. Take care."

Watching him saunter away as if he didn't have a care in the world made Sara feel surprisingly bereft. If he had followed her to town to protect her, why was he leaving? Nobody had been arrested for shooting at her or trashing her apartment, so surely she still needed protection.

But I started this. I'm the one who left him, first, she reminded herself. *All Adam is doing is complying with my stated wishes that he let me make my own choices and handle my life without his interference.*

All of a sudden she realized the magnitude of her error. *Be careful what you wish for*, Vicki used to say. *You might get it.*

Turning his back on Sara had been difficult for Adam. If he had not known that she was being watched almost constantly by the local police and that the owner of the garage was a good, honest man, he didn't think he'd have been able to do it.

He was reaching for the door handle of his truck when he heard her shout, "Adam!" Her voice was high-pitched, very loud and sounded frantic. Wheeling, he ran back to the repair business and skidded to a stop by her side at the customer counter. "What is it? What's wrong?"

The scrap of paper in her hand was quivering so much it was hard to read when she held it out for him, so he grasped her wrist. It took only moments to understand why she had called to him. "Where did you get this?"

Sara gestured over the counter, trembling. "Brad found it on my car this morning."

Adam's eyebrow arched. Brad Babcock was a distant relation to Vicki's grieving family. There were so many Babcocks in Paradise it hadn't occurred to him to take special notice. Besides, Brad had such a great reputation for honesty and skill that nearly everyone took their vehicle repairs to him. Using him to fix up Sara's car was perfectly normal.

"Where was this, exactly?" Adam asked the balding garage owner.

"Tucked under the wipers. I'd a figured it was a prank if I didn't know what happened before."

"Yeah." Adam looked back at the note Sara was still grasping and realized his support of her wrist had become more of a caress. That was not enough to convince him to release her. Instead, he gently tugged on a corner of the note with his free hand until she let go.

"Who else handled this, Brad?"

"Um, pretty much all of us. Junior found it first and showed it to me. Then we passed it around."

"That's what I was afraid of," Adam said. "You got a new plastic bag I can put it into?"

"Sure. Here you go. Sorry I didn't think of doing that right off."

Sara slipped a hand inside the crook of Adam's elbow and hung on as if she needed support to stay on her feet. He glanced at her. Her face was pale, her beautiful eyes wide, her lips slightly parted. So much for her declaration that she didn't need anybody's support.

And no wonder. The note was short and to the point:

The next time I'll use the knife on you.

"We need to give that to the police," Sara finally said after staring at the note through the clear plastic until she couldn't bear to continue.

To her relief, Adam agreed. "Right. Come on. I'll walk you over there and then we'll come back for your car."

This was one time she had to agree with his sensible plan. The combined police and fire department offices were less than half a block away and the sheriff's office was just around the next corner. Walking would be as fast as driving.

Sara pointed to the note as they started out. "Do you think he'll be able to find any forensic clues?"

"That's why I was asking how many people had touched it. I was hoping for clear fingerprints but that's not likely after it was passed around."

"I suppose not." She couldn't help feeling dejected. "It would be nice to catch a break once in a while."

Adam huffed and shook his head. "You think you haven't? What about the times the shooter missed? How about not being in your apartment when it was ransacked? And don't forget Texas. If Vicki really was murdered you could have been, too, if you'd gone with her that night. Your friend Rodrigo didn't come all the way up here just for fun. Be grateful."

Eyes widening, Sara stared at him. "Whoa. Where did all *that* come from?"

"Chalk it up to experience," Adam said. "Nothing

makes a person appreciate survival like walking through fire, so to speak."

Continuing the analogy, Sara said, "I already feel pretty singed around the edges. It's as if every move I make results in another threat or more actual violence." Pausing to take a deep breath and releasing it slowly, she added, "That's why I'm moving back to town and away from your family. I don't want anybody else to get hurt because of me."

"Kurt still insists he fell and hit his head."

She rolled her eyes. "You don't actually believe that fairy tale, do you?"

"I'd like to, but I suspect he's just trying to make you feel better."

Detecting a slump to his broad shoulders she realized he agreed with her analysis, so she put it into words. "I don't care what he says. Somebody was sneaking around your ranch and conked him. We both know that. The question is, who?"

"And why."

"No, Adam. We know why. It happened because of me, because you took me in and tried to protect me. Like I said, that's not going to happen again."

He paused and waved the bag containing the crumpled paper in front of her face. "What about this?"

"What about it?"

"Whoever slashed your tires is threatening to do the same to you. Doesn't that make you even a little nervous?"

Fed up, she fisted her hands on her hips and gritted her teeth before replying. "Of course, it does. It also points out that this person not only knows plenty about me, he's familiar enough with Paradise to move around without being noticed. What does that say to you?"

Keeping her gaze fixed on Adam she waited, analyzing his expression as he struggled with his own conclusion. "You're implying that your attackers have to be locals?"

"It's as likely as having a gang from down south follow me all the way up here."

"I don't buy it. Think, Sara. If the men Miss Bessie saw were tracking Vicki and looking for something in her apartment, the logical thing for them to do is burn it to destroy whatever evidence may have been hidden there."

"Not if they found it."

"Only they couldn't have, could they? Vicki never came home. And she never returned from her trip to the mission office that night during the flood, either."

"You're right," Sara said. "But if they were part of the reason she was killed, then they should also know the evidence against them was washed away when the office floated off."

"Not necessarily. What if they think she passed clues to *you*?"

"And I brought them home with me?" That possibility chilled her to the bone. Could they think she was holding evidence of their crimes? She supposed it was possible. Everybody knew she and Vicki were not only dear friends but also cousins. Sharing important information like that would have made sense.

And, Sara reminded herself, Vicki had told her about her suspicions of theft of goods from the organization. Signatures on receipts proved that far more supplies had been delivered than were properly dispensed or left in inventory. Somebody was making money on the side by selling necessities that were meant for flood victims. And if it was happening in Texas, no telling how many other previous sites had been involved. The question was, had Vicki revealed enough to end the stealing?

Clearing her head of the emotional aspects was critical. The best way she could think of to do that was to keep moving and talk it out with Adam. "I don't remember much," Sara began as she kept pace with his long strides. "I do know it wasn't the theft of monetary donations Vicki was tracing. It was supplies. She'd compared what was left in stock with what had come in and then disbursed to victims, and had come up tons short."

"That happened a lot overseas. It was almost impossible to trace shrinkage."

"I know. That's the rub. If Rigo hadn't shown up in Paradise I wouldn't have suspected his connection."

"Assuming that's why he went to Vicki's."

Frustrated, Sara shook her head. "We have to start assuming some things or we'll get nowhere. Rigo and at least one other man showed up in town and Vicki's place burned down. One or both of them must have lit the fire. There are few other possibilities."

Adam huffed. "I can't help remembering how you lectured me about not jumping to conclusions about strangers."

"That was before people started shooting at me," Sara said. Stating the obvious caused her to edge closer to Adam and scan the quiet town square. "Do you think it's even safe to be out here, exposed like this?"

He pointed to the courthouse in the center of the square on their right. "Court's not in session and it's early for most of these businesses. If we keep our eyes open I doubt anybody can sneak up on us the way they did in the dark."

She rolled her eyes. "Oh, that's comforting."

"It's sensible. I wasn't trying to make you feel too safe. We'll need to stay vigilant." He smiled down at her. "If you think of Paradise as a battle zone until we find out what's going on you should be fine."

"That's the problem," Sara said sadly. "I don't want to view my hometown as a bad place. It's always been a comfort. I could hardly wait to get home from college and go to work at the county hospital."

"I feel the same," Adam told her. "Except I have the experience of seeing the most peaceful third-world villages turned into infernos of death and destruction. No place in the world is totally safe, Sara. No place."

"That is so sad."

He nodded soberly. "Very."

The single dispatcher for fire and police looked up as Adam held the door for Sara, then followed her through into the austere office. Bare fluorescent tubes hung from a dull ceiling, and the walls were painted the same depressing green shade that always reminded him of hospitals. The only real difference was the absence of an antiseptic odor.

Nevertheless, Adam smiled in greeting. "Morning, Ceci. Is the chief in?"

"Morning." She removed her headset, fluffed her short graying hair and jerked a thumb over her shoulder. "Ellis is in his office."

"No, not *my* chief," Adam explained. "We want to talk to the police chief."

"Floyd Magill? What for? You thinkin' of changin' careers?"

"Not today." Adam continued to smile at her rather than explain and invite more rumors involving Sara's troubles. "Is he around?"

"Nope." She glanced at a large clock mounted above an eclectic collection of framed certificates, photos and awards. "It's breakfast time. You'll find him over at the Eden Café. Back booth."

"Thanks," Adam said lightly as he tucked the bagged note into his pocket. He could tell Sara was as nervous as a deer caught in the beam of approaching headlights. She was grasping his arm so tightly he expected his hand to go numb any second. "We'll catch him over there."

This time, Sara straight-armed the door and thrust it far enough open that they could pass through together before it swung shut. Adam didn't protest. He fully understood her desire to speak to the police chief ASAP. Personally, he wanted to unload the note before something happened to it.

They crossed at the street corner. "What if he's finished eating and left?" Sara asked.

"If Floyd isn't there we'll connect with the sheriff again. Either way, the evidence will end up in good hands."

"Do you think anybody will take it seriously?"

Adam refrained from speculation, but he wasn't encouraged about the viability of the note or the methods available in such a small town. If Magill chose to send the clue on to Springfield or, even better, Jefferson City, there might be a chance of tracing the writer. Otherwise, he wasn't going to hold his breath.

And as far as Sara was concerned he still didn't know what to do, how much to insist upon having his way in her daily life. She was one stubborn woman. She had courage beyond many men he'd met, yet her bravado was mixed with an unreasonable sense of being right. Nobody was always right. That's where sensible friends came in. Friends like him.

She paused at the glass door of the storefront café on the east side of the square. The Eden Café wasn't fancy but the food was great, meaning the place was packed at that time of the morning.

Adam reached to open the door for her. She touched his arm. "Wait. I really don't want to face all those people. Half of them probably think I'm the reason Vicki's gone."

"Don't be ridiculous." He wasn't about to openly agree with her regarding town gossip. It could be devastating once the rumor mill got hold of a notion, and the worse the news the more swiftly it traveled.

He slipped an arm around her waist and pulled her to his side. "I'm not leaving you out here alone, Sara. You can walk with me, or I'll sling you over my shoulder in a fireman's carry and we'll go in that way."

"You wouldn't dare." She tried to lean away but he held her fast.

"Look, I left you for just a few minutes this morning and you had to face that threatening note alone. That's not happening again." He gave her a lopsided smile and arched an eyebrow. "Your choice. It might give them something else to talk about if I picked you up and carried you in."

To Adam's relief she giggled. "I'll walk. Let's go."

TEN

Police Chief Magill, clad in a navy blue shirt, pants and a lightweight jacket with the Paradise Police patch on the sleeve, was seated in a rear booth just as the dispatcher had predicted. Keeping focus on their goal so she wouldn't have to make eye contact with others, Sara zigzagged between tables, went straight to him and slid into the unoccupied bench.

Adam followed, choosing her side of the table and blocking any chance of her exiting without first shoving him out of the way. She started to object to the crowding, then thought better of it. Truth to tell, being sandwiched between Adam's broad shoulders and a solid wall was pretty comforting.

The police chief stopped eating and blotted his bushy gray mustache with a paper napkin. "I get the idea this isn't a casual meeting. What's up, folks?"

A lump was clogging Sara's throat. "I—I got a threatening note."

"Show me." He pushed aside his plate.

"Adam has it. We put it in plastic as soon as I got it but lots of people handled it before that."

Magill looked disgusted. "You'd think, with all the CSI stuff on TV, folks would realize they should keep their hands off evidence." He reached out. "Let me see."

Adam obliged. "Brad, over at the garage, found it stuck under her windshield wiper when he opened this morning. He said they'd passed it around the shop and everybody working there had touched it. He gave us this plastic bag to put it in but it was probably too late by then."

"Probably. Still, this scrap of paper looks like it was torn from something bigger. Maybe that will give us a clue." Pausing, he glanced across the table at Sara. "Anything else?"

"Well," she said, "I do remember that Vicki kept a diary. If you can get a peek at that you might uncover some clues, maybe a motive, in case her drowning wasn't an accident. She thought she'd uncovered theft so it's possible someone down there decided to get rid of her. If the diary wasn't washed away in the flood it may have been sent home to her mother with her other personal belongings."

"I can ask," the chief replied. "If Helen chooses to give it to me, fine. If not, there's nothing I can do legally. Texas police have declared Vicki's death an accident."

Sara sighed noisily. "Oh."

"You taking care, Miz Sara?"

She hesitated, then spoke her mind. "Trying to. I did it Adam's way and all that accomplished was getting a lump on his brother's head. I don't intend to act foolishly, but I am going back to work. My hospital has door guards and cameras in all the hallways, plus plans for defense in the event of an attack. I can't think of anyplace I'd be safer."

Adam humphed. "How about away from the public?"

"Like last night?" she said with a touch of cynicism. "That worked well."

"We had a visitor out at the ranch," Adam explained in reply to the chief's raised eyebrows. "They apparently drove off when we left to take Kurt to ER."

"Whoa. The sheriff's department didn't mention getting a call out your way."

"Probably because the threat passed and we drove Kurt to the hospital. By that time..."

Floyd interrupted. "Hold on. Start from the beginning."

As Adam explained the previous night's drama in detail, Sara had to stifle a strong urge to contribute comments. It wasn't that Adam was leaving anything out. She simply felt compelled to offer her personal opinion.

However, when Adam finished explaining and Floyd looked to her for corroboration, she merely nodded.

The chief pushed his plate away, drained the last dregs of his coffee, blotted his mustache again and got to his feet, hat in hand. "Okay. I'll get this sent off to the state lab, just in case. In the meantime, I'd advise you two to keep a low profile." He looked to Sara as he donned his official cap. "I see no reason for you to miss work. Just watch your back and don't get complacent."

"Wait a minute." Adam stood to face the chief. "There's no way I can keep an eye on her if she goes back to work."

"Then I guess you'll have to settle for escorting her to and from."

Sara realized the seriousness of her situation, yet the astonished expression on Adam's face almost made her chuckle. He was so used to calling the shots and getting his own way, it was amusing to see him reacting to an opposite result.

Taking pity, she grasped his hand as she slid out of the booth and joined the men. "I'll be fine. Really I will."

Adam looked decidedly unhappy. "I don't like it."

This obvious comment encouraged her to smile. She gave Adam's fingers a squeeze when she looked up at him and sweetly said, "Tough."

To her surprise his gaze darkened, his eyes narrowed and he glared at her. She'd assumed he'd find dark humor in her comment so to see him get angry came as a shock. So did the rest of his behavior. After a moment's pause he jerked his hand out of her grasp, wheeled and headed for the exit.

A hush came over the dining area. Sara's jaw dropped. Where had all that fury come from? One minute Adam had been promising to defend her against the whole world and the next he was stomping through the door and into the street.

"You sure pulled the bit tight on his bridle," Floyd said with a grin that lifted the ends of his mustache.

"Sure looks like it."

The chief's laugh echoed inside the small café, bouncing off the wood-paneled walls and causing murmurs among the other diners. Sara was painfully aware that Adam had caused a scene, leaving her and Magill to deal with unwanted attention. She was not pleased. Not one bit.

"Did you get your car back after you found the note?" the lawman asked.

Sara shook her head. "No. We left it at the garage and came to find you."

"Then I'll walk you back over to pick up the car." He gestured toward the door where they'd last seen Adam. "Unless you'd rather chase after your cowboy."

"He's not my cowboy," she grumbled. Her eyes to the floor, she hurried to escape all the stares and whispers. She couldn't help thinking, *Adam is not my anything*, and wondering if he still considered her even a friend. Before today she had never seen him display that kind of swift anger or show such a lack of self-control.

The chief accompanied her to the door and out onto the sidewalk before he commented. "Kane takes pride in his work and his life's goals. We men do that. Don't sell him short, Miz Sara. He's one of the good ones."

"I know that." Shading her eyes from the morning sun she peered up at him. "Why did he get so mad? I was only teasing him the same as I used to when we were kids. It never bothered him before."

Steve was smiling as he looked her up and down. "If you don't mind an old man saying so, you're no kid now, Sara. And Adam isn't a shy teenage boy, either. You can't treat him like one and get away with it. Not anymore."

"I wasn't. I didn't…" But she had and she knew it. No wonder Adam kept acting as if she were his childhood buddy. She was unconsciously perpetuating that concept herself.

Sara made a face and glanced at her companion. The cut of his police uniform gave him an air of authority and helped mask his love of food, but it was nothing like seeing Adam in his fire department garb. Or dressed for ranch work, come to think of it. No matter what Adam Kane wore, which profession he personified, he was the most ruggedly handsome man she'd ever seen. And the most appealing.

Someday, maybe, when he wasn't in a huff, she'd tell him so. Today, however, was clearly not the right time.

Adam didn't go far. He rounded the corner nearest the café and waited. Why did that woman get under his skin so easily? And why was he having so much trouble keeping an even temper no matter what Sara said or did? The answer was plain. He was desperately worried about her safety and cared way too much for his own good. Having her thwart his plans to protect her and then joke about it had pushed him too far because he was so frustrated with her and with their situation.

Further reflection reminded Adam that Sara was behaving the same way he was. Was she on edge for the same reasons? Was it possible she, too, was sensing the kind of personal attraction to him that he was developing for her? Was that why she kept seesawing between camaraderie and pushing him away?

His pulse jumped like a wild mustang when he spotted her crossing the town square in the company of the police chief. Well, at least she'd kept her head enough to allow someone to escort her. That was smart. So why was she so determined to keep *him* at arm's length?

Assuming that Sara was headed back to the B Street Garage to claim her car, Adam circled around to his pickup truck and moved it to where he could observe her without calling attention to himself. Since she wouldn't allow him to openly guard her, he'd have to do his best on the sly. What he was going to do when it was time for him to go back to twenty-four-hour shifts at the fire department he didn't know, but this would suffice for the time being.

Magill escorted Sara to the garage office and went in with her. Adam watched and fidgeted. The chief couldn't have stayed inside for more than two or three minutes before leaving. That meant Sara was now on her own again.

Adam was considering getting out of his truck to be closer to her when he saw her familiar small car leaving the lot. She didn't turn toward him but that didn't matter. There were only two places she was likely to go: her new house or the hospital. Both could be reached easily from the center of Paradise, so he started by plotting a course for the closest rather than chase her through the streets and be noticed.

Wheeling into the co-op parking lot to access her new home, he pulled behind an enormous trash receptacle, parked and got out. "Sara, Sara, Sara, where are you?" He knew she wasn't scheduled to work, so the logical choice had been to stake out the small house Cynthia had found for her. Apparently, he had chosen wrong.

Adam slipped his cell phone out of his pocket to check the time. Given his agitated emotional state it was possible he'd imagined how long it should take her to get there. Barely three minutes had passed since he'd left his truck.

He scanned the area around the small house again.

And saw movement!

Could Sara have parked on the opposite side street and entered through the rear yard? He supposed it was possible even if it was the least sensible choice. He took a step forward. Then another. Something was wrong. Whoever was circling the perimeter of the dwelling wasn't walking normally. He or she was acting furtively.

Since he was still holding his cell he punched her unlisted number on his contact list. She answered almost immediately. "Hello?"

"Sara, it's me. Adam. Where are you?"

"Stop worrying. I'm fine, okay?"

His voice was low and gravelly because he didn't want to be overheard. "Where are you?"

"If you must know, I'm on my way to buy new clothes," she said, sounding a trifle put out.

"You didn't go to your new place?"

"No. Why?"

"Because I see somebody messing around outside it. Looks like they're trying to find an unlocked window. I thought maybe you'd misplaced your keys."

"I haven't had time to stop at Cynthia's to pick them up yet. You should know that. You were with me almost all morning."

"Right. Listen," Adam said, "I'm going to go see who it is and what they want. If I don't call you back in five minutes, call the police."

"Adam!" Her shout was so piercing he held the phone away from his ear.

"Just do it."

"Why wait?" she demanded. Adam could picture her facing him down, hands on her hips, eyes blazing.

"Because if I call and the person hears sirens or even suspects I've seen him, he'll run. We need to stop this right now and find out who it is."

"You're a firefighter, not a cop."

"I'm also a marine."

"That doesn't make you bulletproof."

Adam chuckled under his breath, relieved to hear concern from Sara, especially considering their recent tiffs. "You sound as though you might care if I got shot."

"Of *course* I would, you stubborn—"

"Now, now, watch your language, Miz Southerland."

She made a noise that sounded like a combination of disgust and frustration. "The only time I have any trouble being nice is when I'm around you. Wait for me. I'm coming."

Of course Adam couldn't allow her to join him until he had cleared the area but he didn't say so. He simply ended their conversation, tucked the phone back into his pocket and started jogging toward the semi-isolated dwelling.

The shadowy figure he'd been observing stopped moving for an instant, then dashed around the corner of the building.

Adam broke into a run.

Followed the path of the suspect.

Swung around the same corner.

And hit the ground face first.

* * *

Sara wheeled into the co-op parking lot, spotted Adam's truck and skidded to a stop next to it. Where was he?

Not knowing which way to go she paused and studied the scene. There was no way to tell where he had gone or whether or not he was all right. She gritted her teeth. "If anything bad happens to you because of me, Adam Kane, I'll never forgive you."

Sadly, her life consisted of many acquaintances yet only two true friends. Losing Vicki had been bad enough. Losing Adam, too, would be… It was unthinkable.

Starting off at a brisk pace, Sara approached the rear of the tiny dwelling. Shade trees had shed fall leaves and they were piled up in heaps against the rear wall. A few branches showed new buds but right now the old walnut tree and its oak companions cast gnarled shadows that reminded her of spooky fall pictures.

Traffic in the nearby street continued to hum. Birds that should have been singing spring's praises and flitting overhead, however, were silent. So were the insects.

Should she call out to Adam? No. That would be foolish if the threat she was sensing was real. But she could use her phone. Surely Adam had switched his cell to vibrate for safety.

Her hands were shaking as she cradled the smartphone. His cell number was easily located. She tapped the screen, put the instrument to her ear and waited. It started ringing. Echoing.

Echoing? Sara held her breath and strained to listen. His cell phone was sounding off, all right, only what she was hearing wasn't coming from their connection. It was coming from the other side of the building!

"Adam?"

There was no reply. Trembling so badly she could hardly stand she pocketed her phone as she cast around for a weapon. Anything she could lay her hands on would do.

A brittle, broken tree branch seemed to be the only option so she scooped it up, raised it like a baseball bat and started toward the sound of the ring tones.

Something rustled in the fallen leaves ahead. Sara whipped around the corner, branch held high, and came upon him. Breath left her in a whoosh. Her defensive stance held while she looked for others and demanded, "What are you doing? Why didn't you answer your phone?"

Then she noticed the dry leaves he was brushing from his hair and clothing as he sat up. "What happened? Were you hit? Shot? What? Answer me!"

He huffed as he stood and continued to clean, leaning forward to ruffle his short dark hair. "Beats me."

"How did you end up covered with leaves?"

Stretching and obviously mentally checking himself over he shook his head. "I guess I ran into something that knocked the wind out of me." He rubbed his stomach. "I didn't see a thing."

"That wouldn't be enough to keep you down and out." She cast aside the crumbly dead limb she'd been carrying as a weapon and dusted off her hands.

"That's what I thought."

"When did you get here?"

"I'd just arrived when I phoned you. Why?"

"Because that was five or six minutes ago. A blow to the torso shouldn't have caused unconsciousness unless you have internal bleeding. And in that case you would probably still be lying on the ground." She reached toward him. "Let me check."

Adam took a step back and wobbled. "I'm fine."

"Look, I'm the expert here. Stop arguing and stand still so I can be sure."

He ended up leaning against the side of the wooden building while she gently examined his neck, shoulder and rib areas. Other than a chuckle when she inadvertently tickled him, he didn't comment.

Feeling light-headed, Sara managed to keep her mind on her task only because she was so concerned for his health and welfare. By the time she finished the cursory exam she was fighting the urge to throw her arms around him in relief that he was okay.

Instead, she stepped back. "I'm not finding a thing wrong with you. No broken ribs. Are you sure you weren't hit on the head?"

Adam put a hand to his forehead and started to shake his head, then stopped. "No, but I am kind of dizzy. What smells funny?"

He sniffed his hand, then extended it toward her. "What's this odor?"

She gasped. "No wonder I was having trouble getting my breath. I thought maybe I was having an allergy attack. Somebody used ether to knock you out after you were down!"

"I must have fought them and got some on my hands."

"Apparently. It's old-fashioned but effective."

"That's crazy. Who runs around with a bottle of ether in their pocket?"

That question sent a shiver zinging up Sara's spine despite the warmth of the sun. "Someone who plans to incapacitate another person, namely me, since this is my new home."

The stern expression on Adam's face told her all she needed to know. He agreed. And he was getting ready to issue more marching orders, orders she was loathe to accept.

Why not listen to his advice? Why not let him boss her around? What was it about their history that made her act so independent and resist his guidance?

A surprising answer popped into her head and she nearly rejected it out of hand. Could she be holding a grudge about his leaving town right after her high school graduation? They'd had plans for the future, at least she'd had. And Adam had totally rejected both her ideas and herself. Watching him leave had plunged a hypothetical knife into her heart. Seeing him kiss and hug Vicki goodbye had twisted it until she'd fled rather than see any more.

So, if she was withholding forgiveness the problem was hers. So was the decision whether or not to deal with it.

Something told her it would have been easier if she wasn't being stalked and threatened. Then again, if these trying circumstances had not thrown Adam and her together, perhaps she would never have faced the truth. Up against a possible end to her life, petty disappointments of the past seemed inconsequential.

Why was that? she wondered as her thoughts whirled.

She huffed in disgust. Because in the grand scheme of things, they didn't matter at all.

Making eye contact with Adam before he had a chance to speak again she blinked back tears and simply said, "I'm so sorry."

ELEVEN

Adam had absolutely no idea why Sara was apologizing but he was savvy enough to accept. "Don't worry about it. A little dizziness is a small price to pay for looking after you."

"That wasn't what I meant." She was clearly unhappy as she waved her hands in the air between them, then said, "Never mind. We need to make a police report even though you say there's no lasting damage. One of these days this guy is going to make a mistake and really hurt somebody."

"I'll do it. You stay put."

She made a cynical face at him. "I may be opinionated at times but I'm not crazy, Adam. I'm not going anywhere. Call Floyd."

Adam was put through to the chief who was traveling in a patrol car. "Magill."

"I'm over here behind the co-op with Sara," Adam explained. "I was waiting for her at her new digs and somebody hit me and then knocked me out with ether."

"How do you know?"

"We can both smell it," Adam said. "I must have gotten some on my hands when I was trying to keep it off my face."

"I'm in that neighborhood so I'll cover the call myself.

Was there more than one person involved in the attack?" the chief asked.

"I don't know. I don't remember much except hitting the ground, struggling a little and waking up feeling dizzy. Why?"

"Because you're a big, strong guy. I can't see one assailant keeping you down long enough to gas you."

"Something did knock the air out of me first. Sara says no ribs are broken but my side sure smarts."

"Should I start an ambulance?"

"No," Adam insisted. "I have my own nurse on scene."

The chief laughed. "I don't know that I'd let her hear you say that."

"Too late." Adam used his free arm to pull her to his good side and hold her there. "You were on speaker."

"And she's not chewing you out? Well, well, will wonders never cease."

"All right, you two," she said flatly. "That's enough teasing. We need to get serious before this escalates more than it already has."

Adam sobered, keeping her tucked close. "She's right, Chief. We'll wait in my truck. See you soon." He ended the call.

"My car," Sara countered. "It has windows."

"Picky, picky." Adam accompanied her to where both vehicles waited. He scanned their surroundings over the top of her small sedan and sheltered her with his body as he'd done before. "Let's get in so we can talk."

"Fine. Seeing you covered in dry leaves was enough of a shock to trigger extra adrenaline and it's starting to wear off."

He opened the door to the back seat for her, then circled the car and slid in himself before he said, "Something you just told the chief has me thinking."

"I hope it's led you to conclusions because constantly being on edge has me jumping at shadows. Literally."

"Okay. See what you think. Consider the escalation. These attacks started with the fire at Vicki's. Right? You didn't notice anything odd before that?"

"Other than so-called friends avoiding me like the plague? No, I can't say I did." She paused to sigh and leaned back against the seat. "Some of that may have been my problem, not theirs. I came home drowning in guilt and may have projected my own feelings onto innocent situations. I really don't know."

Adam reached for her hand, relieved when she permitted him to hold it. "Break it down with me. The gunshots were first, at the fire and later in town. Yes?"

"Yes."

"Plus, we found your trashed apartment over the insurance office on the square."

"Right."

"Assuming that had to have happened while you were volunteering at the fire, we may be dealing with unconnected events."

"Not necessarily."

"But possibly?" He was relieved to see her nod. "Okay, so say the minor stuff is happening because of one faction and the really dangerous attacks are due to another. Are you with me so far?"

"I'm with you but I'm not exactly thrilled. Do you really think I'm on *two* hit lists?"

It wouldn't do her any good if he downplayed his conclusions so he was blunt. "At least two. Maybe more. Damage with paint and slashed tires and stalking is one thing. Shooting at you is another."

"They keep missing." The hopefulness in her expression made him sorry he felt so strongly about going on.

"They may be trying to frighten you," Adam suggested. "Or they're terrible shots. Either way, any of those bullets could have hit you. Red paint is merely a nuisance. You can *die* from being shot."

"Well, duh."

His fingers tightened around hers. "I'm not saying all this to scare you, Sara. I've been over and over it in my head and there's really no other plausible explanation. You have multiple stalkers."

She was shaking her head. "No. Stop saying that. I haven't done anything to deserve being harassed and attacked. I've spent my entire adult life helping people."

"And you've done a marvelous job of it. I know that. So do your real friends. It's the confused element that is overlooking all the good you've done, plus criminals who've apparently followed you to Paradise for their own reasons. I think the first thing we need to do is try to solve the mystery behind whatever Vicki uncovered. That may tell us why Rodrigo was killed, too."

"How?"

Adam could feel tremors from her arm to her fingertips. "We can start by seeing what the police found out about a diary or journal. You're positive Vicki kept one?"

"Yes. I know. I teased her about it."

"You're sure she had it with her in Texas?"

"I think so. I hope so. I was so used to seeing her writing something I hardly paid attention."

Adam looked up when flashing blue and red lights swung into the lot beside them. "Okay. Here's our first move. If Caruthers or Magill have approached Helen, they may already have our answer."

The slight smile she bestowed on him nearly melted his heart, particularly when she said, "That's what I've been praying for."

* * *

Expecting Adam to order her to remain in the car, Sara had prepared a clever and firm rebuttal. When he simply climbed out she followed in silence.

The police chief shook Adam's hand, then hers when she offered it. "Everybody really okay here?"

"I'm fine." She inclined her head toward Adam. "Him, I'm not so sure of. I thought he was okay but I saw him wince just now when he stood up."

"Well, he's a big boy and you're a medical professional so I'll let you two settle it." He looked to Adam. "What went on out here? Did you get a good look at the prowler?"

"No," Adam said. "Just shadows."

"And by the time I got here I didn't see anything but Adam, getting up and brushing off leaves." Sara paused for a quick glance at the stalwart man standing so comfortingly close. "We didn't see any point of entry but couldn't check the inside for ourselves because I haven't picked up the key from Cynthia Weatherly yet."

"Okay. I'll have one of my deputies stop by her office and get it on his way over with an evidence kit. Anything else you can tell me?"

Sara watched Adam shaking his head as she did the same. "What about Vicki's diary?" she asked. "Did you or the sheriff have a chance to speak to her mom about it?"

Magill huffed. "Oh, I spoke to her all right. I was glad I did it on the phone instead of standing there asking in person. She almost bit my head off. Finally, her son, Will, took the receiver from her and calmed her down. I haven't heard salty language like Helen's since my days in the navy."

Blanching, Sara shivered. Most of the time Helen Babcock acted like a mild-mannered, churchgoing Southern lady. To hear that she had spoken so rudely to the chief was not only a shock, it was a big disappointment. Grief was to blame, of course. Losing a child, even an adult child, had to be the worst trauma any parent could experience. In retrospect, Sara was glad Aunt Helen had refrained from giving her the same kind of dressing down at the funeral.

Magill used his radio to request backup and give the necessary orders, then turned to Sara and Adam. "You two can hang around if you want but I see no reason for it. My men and I'll handle things here. Why don't you go grab lunch or something?"

"Meaning you want to get us out from underfoot?" she asked with a smile. "Okay. And thanks for everything. Come on, Adam. I still need to shop for new clothes and you may as well go along."

"You don't mind?"

"Not at all."

His left brow arched and he peered down at her. "What's the catch?"

She waggled both her brows and smiled. "You're pretty smart for a cowboy."

"Well, they didn't hit me in the head the way they did Kurt."

"True. I'm sure that's a plus." She laid the back of her hand on his forehead to make sure he didn't feel feverish. "Actually, since you've insisted you don't need to go to ER as a precaution, I intend to stick like glue until I'm sure you're okay."

"You don't believe me when I tell you I'm not hurting that badly?"

"Oh, I believe you, up to a point. I also know you're a typical macho man. A marine. A rough, tough cowboy and fearless firefighter. What are the chances you may be underestimating an injury?"

Snorting a chuckle he smiled. "Fair to good, since you put it that way."

Sara linked her arm with his and urged him back toward her car. "I thought so. Come on. I'm driving."

Given her willingness to stay with him he decided it was wisest to follow her orders. At least they had been delivered with good humor instead of barked the way a drill sergeant might. The only thing still puzzling him was Sara's apology that had come out of nowhere. Since she was currently acting friendly and compliant he decided to postpone asking for an explanation. Finding out would wait. Being in her company, for whatever reason, was a definite bonus, one he did not intend to spoil.

As she left the co-op parking lot he settled back in his seat. "So, where are we going?"

"Shopping, then lunch."

"You're not going to drive all the way to the outlet mall in Branson, are you?"

"I wasn't planning to but that's a good idea."

"For another time, maybe?" He fidgeted.

Sara laughed as she cast him a sidelong glance. "Yes, for another time. I meant it about keeping an eye on your condition. I want to stick pretty close to the hospital in case the blow to your ribs damaged your liver or spleen."

"Come on, Sara. Do you honestly think it did?"

"No. But there's no sense taking chances. My daily life is already too supercharged. I don't want a medical emergency on my hands, too."

"Sorry about miscalculating. Judging by the way the shadow was moving I thought he'd be long gone when I rounded that corner." He huffed with disgust. "Good thing we aren't in a combat zone or I'd be a goner."

Her hands fisted on the steering wheel. "Maybe we should pretend we are. I won't know how to behave that defensively but you can teach me."

Adam swallowed a chuckle. "You want me to give you marine training?"

"Self-defense, maybe. It can't hurt, can it?"

"Hand-to-hand fighting is a skill that takes practice. It's not learned in a couple of lessons." *Besides*, he added to himself, *the less you know, the less likely you'll be to rush into a dangerous situation*.

"I'm not asking for proficiency. All I want you to do is show me a few simple moves, like how to get away if somebody grabs me."

"Ha. If they do, make sure they aren't carrying ether." Slowly shaking his head he chastised himself for carelessness. "It was my fault I was knocked out, Sara. Being here in Paradise is so different than fighting in battle that I got too complacent."

He was looking directly at her when she turned for a moment and met his gaze. The blue of her eyes glistened. Her jaw was set. Worry furrowed her brow.

"It isn't safe here. Not for me, for us," she said with conviction. "We're in a battle of good versus evil whether we like it or not and we have to win. We just have to."

Adam reached across and laid a hand of comfort on her shoulder when he warned, "Sometimes that's easier said than done."

TWELVE

The big box store Sara chose to visit was handy, meaning it would do until she could shop elsewhere and find more variety. To her delight, Adam seemed to be feeling as well as he'd claimed. That didn't mean she was going to part from him, of course; it was simply a current blessing.

Which was exactly what his presence was, she concluded. A blessing. A huge, sweet, adorable blessing. Of course she'd never put those feelings into words but that didn't mean she couldn't privately bask in their comfort. This was one of the things that confused her. A terrible tragedy had brought this amazingly deepened closeness to the man she'd loved for as long as she could remember. It seemed wrong to be so happy when Vicki's death was so fresh, yet she couldn't help herself.

A Scripture promise from the fifth chapter of the book of Matthew popped into her head: "Blessed are they that mourn: for they shall be comforted." Was that why she wasn't weeping all the time? Maybe. She was certainly mourning in her deepest heart even if it didn't always show in her outward actions. Perhaps that was one reason why some of the townspeople thought she was callous or had had something to do with her cousin's death. That thought was sad in many ways, primarily because it meant they didn't understand the kind of comfort and healing her Christian faith provided.

She wheeled into the first available space near the door. "You're coming in, right?"

"Wouldn't miss it for the world," Adam said with a wry smile. "I have always wondered why women fussed the way they do when jeans, boots, a plaid shirt and a Stetson are all anybody needs to wear."

Sara laughed softly. "And a work uniform. Scrubs are mainly what I need right now."

"You're still determined to go back to work?"

"Absolutely. I have to work to eat and afford my rent. Besides, if I don't carry on as usual, that may convince the bad guys I have a reason to hide."

"I've been giving that some thought." He climbed out of the car and fell into step beside her. "I wonder if you or I could convince Helen Babcock to share Vicki's diary."

"Assuming it was sent home to her, you mean?"

"Yes. I doubt she'd have gotten so mad at the chief if she didn't have it."

"Who knows? The poor thing is grief-stricken," Sara reminded him. "If Floyd didn't approach her with enough compassion he may not have even gotten around to asking to see the journal."

"I think he said he had."

"Whatever." Sara walked through the automatic doors and headed for a line of empty shopping carts.

Adam passed her. "I'll get us a buggy. You just concentrate on picking your new clothes so we can get out of here."

"You have a lot to learn about women and shopping," she quipped.

"That's probably true."

He followed with the squeaky-wheeled cart until she

began to wander between racks of clothing and he ended up in her way.

"Back off a little? Please? I need to be able to walk all the way around these displays."

"Why? If you see what you like, just buy it."

"Says the man who looks as if he always wears the same pair of jeans in various states of wear."

"My shirts are different."

"Mostly the color," she teased. "Otherwise, you're a cookie-cutter cowboy."

"And that's a bad thing?"

She had to laugh again. "I didn't say that. I just like variety, that's all." Sobering as she looked him up and down she added, "I think you look great."

"Thanks. You're not bad yourself. Missy loaned you some nice jeans, at least."

"Yes, and I want to get them laundered and back to her as soon as possible. Remind me to buy a pair of those, too."

With her focus on the rows of scrub tops she relaxed and let Adam watch her back. One or two quick glances proved he was doing just that.

Soon, she had an armload of scrub pants to coordinate with the tops already piled in the cart. "I'm just going to run and try these on," Sara told him. "I'm sure about the tops fitting but not these bottoms."

"Knock yourself out. I'll wait."

"And you are still feeling all right? No nausea or dizziness?"

"Nope. I'm finer than frog hair, as they say."

Sara chuckled quietly. "Nobody says that these days."

"My grandpa used to. Remember him? He could play a mean banjo, even with arthritis crippling up his hands."

"When we were kids. I do remember his playing." She

sighed. "Sometimes I wish we lived in the simpler times he enjoyed, until I think of all the medical breakthroughs that have been made since then."

"In firefighting, too. We're much safer with modern gear."

"But never invincible. That's what I worry about when I see you and the others running into a burning building the way they did at Vicki's."

"Miss Bessie's glad we made entry."

Sara sobered. "I didn't mean it was wrong. I just worry."

"What about trusting God?"

"Yeah, there is that." As they talked she was leading the way toward the center of the ladies' clothing department where the dressing rooms were located. A clerk unlocked one for her and with a last look at Adam she went in.

Trusting God? The last thing she wanted to do was act as if she didn't. In her mind, however, there was a big difference between trusting the Lord and being careless. Surely God didn't expect His children to risk their lives if there was any other way to accomplish a goal.

Sara sighed. Therein lay the answer. Sometimes it was necessary to take chances when that was the only option for the good of others. To be the person you were intended to be. To make the most of one's brief time on earth.

Slipping on the first pair of pants she checked herself in the dressing room mirror, satisfied she'd chosen the right size. As she redressed, her mind refused to let go of thoughts involving her trip to Texas. Had she failed a God-given mission when she hadn't accompanied her cousin on that last foray into the raging waters? Had her own fear held her back when she should have acted? The possibility was enough to bring tears to her eyes.

"Okay, knock it off," Sara told herself. She didn't want anyone to catch her crying. It had been bad enough when Adam had seen her tears. She certainly was not going to permit a public sobfest. Sniffling and swiping at her damp cheeks she slipped her shoes on, checked to make sure her credit card was still in her pocket, gathered up the items she'd decided to buy and left the dressing room.

Another door across from her was also opening. She barely noted its occupant until a woman's voice screeched, "You!"

Sara stumbled to a stop. Her jaw dropped. And the tears she'd thought were under control began to course down her flushed cheeks.

"Aunt Helen, I'm so, so sorry."

The older woman's arms opened as if offering a hug. Sara started forward, all the while weeping.

When she got within reach, Helen drew back and slapped Sara's cheek so hard it felt as if she'd plunged a hundred sharp needles into the tender flesh.

Sara instinctively covered her face with both hands. The loose clothing went flying. Helen screamed epithets and launched into a full-blown attack, swinging, slapping and pummeling Sara with her fists.

Filled with remorse and guilt, deserved or not, Sara ducked and took the punishment without lifting a hand in her own defense.

Adam knew it couldn't be Sara he was hearing. Even at her worst she'd never have used such unacceptable language. However, given her latest problems, he did suspect she was somehow involved.

He abandoned the shopping cart and hurried toward the disturbance. A female clerk in a blue vest tried to stop him. "You can't go in there, sir. It's ladies only."

"Sounds like somebody'd better have a look," he countered, pushing past her. A melee was taking place in a corner of the hallway leading to the row of dressing rooms. The person screaming and flailing was an older woman who was bent over a slim figure curled into a fetal position. *Sara!* Helen Babcock had Sara down and was beating her.

It took only one of Adam's muscular arms encircling the attacker's waist to stop the carnage. He held Helen facing away from him, kicking and screaming, and used his free hand to reach out to Sara.

She was trembling, gasping and sobbing so much she acted as though she didn't even see him. "Sara? It's okay now. I've stopped her."

Although he had, he wasn't sure what he was going to do with his struggling prisoner until he spotted Will Babcock hurrying toward him. "Mother!" The younger man drew back a fist. "Let go of her!"

"I will as soon as she stops trying to beat up Sara," Adam said, gladly passing the hysterical woman to her strapping son.

The moment he was free of that burden, Adam kneeled beside Sara and gently cupped her shoulders, lifting her chin to make her look at him. "I'm here, honey. It's over. You're safe."

Hope and relief filled her expression despite the redness of her face and copious tears. "Adam!"

"Can you stand up?"

"I—I think so."

Cradling her beside him he caressed her damp cheeks. "Are you okay?"

All she did was nod her head and sniffle. A concerned clerk handed her a wad of tissues.

"Are you hurt?" Adam asked.

"N-no. She just caught me off guard."

"Why didn't you fight back?"

"Against Helen? I couldn't. I practically grew up at her house with Vicki. It would be like hitting my own mother."

"Still..." Adam glared at the older woman, now collapsed in her son's arms. "We should call the police."

Sara was adamant. "No. Don't."

Helen behaved as if she was now numb but Will had plenty to say. "The police? Haven't you done enough to my family? Look at my poor mother. You've destroyed her."

Adam pulled Sara closer, sensing her need for physical as well as emotional support. "She didn't do anything to you or your family, Will. Criminals in Texas may have but Sara had nothing to do with that."

"She was there. She should have protected my little sister. They were supposed to be friends."

"They were very close," Adam countered. "If you'll look in your sister's diary and read the pages from the time she and Sara were on the mission trip, maybe you'll understand about the thefts she uncovered."

"Oh, sure. Blame it on fictitious crooks. Anything but put the blame where it belongs."

"Read the book, Will. And when you have, turn it over to the police the way the chief asked."

"What do you mean?"

"Chief Magill approached your mother with a request to examine your sister's journal. She read him the riot act and turned him down." He eyed Helen's shaking shoulders. Her face was buried against Will's chest and, although she had stopped screeching, she was obviously still very distraught.

"I'm not going to dishonor Vicki by letting the public read her private thoughts. No way."

"Not even when doing it might point to her killer?"

"My sister drowned. Period."

"Are you sure?"

"The death certificate says so."

Adam was nodding. He felt Sara's arms tightening around his waist and sensed that she was recovering, so he gave her time to join the conversation. When she didn't, he went on. "What if she was murdered for something she uncovered while she was taking inventory of supplies for the group?"

"That's ridiculous."

"Maybe. Maybe not." Adam stared at the other man, willing him to listen. "You'll never know for sure unless you look at Vicki's notes. We think that's what the arsonists were after when they torched your sister's rental and almost killed Bessie Alt in the process."

Will's arms were still around his mother, comforting her, but he was clearly antagonistic toward anyone else. "That place blew up because Bessie had oxygen tanks inside. You think I don't read the papers?"

"What makes you think journalists know everything? Huh? The police keep facts to themselves even after cases are solved, and Vicki's case is far from it. Just look, that's all we ask."

"We? I should have known," Will countered with a sneer. "Everybody used to call you, Sara and Vicki the Three Musketeers. Too bad you let my sister die."

Adam felt Sara shudder against him. He knew she was innocent but the stigma remained. It would never go away until and unless the Babcock family publically forgave her, and even then there would probably be diehard critics who would never believe in her innocence.

Why had *he* come to believe in her unquestionable innocence? He had no answer. Maybe he never would. But he knew in his heart that she'd have acted to save her dear cousin if she'd seen any way to do so. That was good enough for Adam.

Now all he had to do was make it be enough for all the others. He thought he'd won over the police and sheriff to his point of view and most of his fellow firefighters probably supported her, too, since she was an active volunteer medic. It was the lay population of Paradise who still needed convincing.

He clenched his jaw as he stared at the Babcocks. *Find the journal and read it, Will,* Adam thought, wishing he could project those ideas directly into the man's brain.

Although a sparse crowd had gathered when the melee was going on, people were now starting to disperse. On the fringes of the ladies' wear department, small groups whispered among themselves. Mothers protected children. Husbands shooed curious wives down the nearest aisles.

The more the area cleared, the more Adam relaxed. Sara was dabbing at the last of her tears, taking shuddering breaths and blowing her nose. A clerk had gathered up the new clothes she'd dropped when Helen had attacked her and put them in a cart. Things were settling down. Which is probably why he noticed the one anomaly.

A lone man was standing apart from everyone else and staring at them across the racks of clothes. He was young, muscular and dressed as casually as everyone else, yet there was something off about him.

Adam met his gaze. Sized him up. Attempted to memorize his rugged features, noting the tattoos visible on his neck and forearms. Was he just another curious shopper? Maybe. But if he was, where was his shopping cart?

Adam nudged Sara. "Look, honey. Over there."

"What? Where?" She sniffled again.

He pointed with a tilt of his head and a lift of his chin. "There. That guy. Do you recognize him?"

As Sara turned to look, Adam did, too. The aisle was empty. The man was gone.

"Who?"

"I thought I saw a stranger, that's all. Forget about it." But Adam wouldn't forget. The menacing image of the man he'd spotted was burned into his brain. If he saw him again he'd know him in an instant.

A shiver shot up Adam's spine. It wasn't merely the chance of seeing that man again. He had to see him *first*.

Before the guy had an opportunity to get close enough to harm Sara.

THIRTEEN

Sara was so spent from the ordeal in the store she was going to abandon her garment choices until Adam stepped in. "You may as well go ahead and buy the stuff. It will save us another trip to the store."

Us. That sounded good, particularly after he'd had to come to her rescue again. Poor Helen had never been one of the people she'd feared so the attack had come as a shock. Oh, she could understand why the older woman had lost control. It wasn't that. She'd simply misjudged how Helen might act. If they hadn't accidentally run into each other so soon, Vicki's mother might have had time to progress through her grief and not react so violently.

But they had met. And the result had been so upsetting Sara wanted to bury her face in her hands, start crying and never stop. At one time she'd believed she and Helen were close. Like family, even. So to have her screaming accusations and hysterically hitting made Sara so sad she could hardly bear it. That kind of punishment from a stranger would not have hurt nearly as much.

Moving in a fog of emotions and relying on Adam to shepherd her out of the store, Sara was in the parking lot almost before she knew it.

He looped the handles of the plastic bags around his wrist and held out his hand. "Car keys?"

"Huh? Oh." She reached into her pocket. "Here."

"Where to next?"

Sighing, she settled herself in the passenger seat. "I don't know. I don't really care right now."

"Gotcha. We were going to have lunch. What sounds good?"

Her dry wit pushed its way up from her subconscious and made her say, "Crow?"

"Don't beat yourself up, Sara. You didn't do anything wrong, before or since Texas."

"I keep telling myself that, so why do I feel so guilty?"

"Because you have a heart for others. You care. That's probably what led you to become a nurse. I have the same problem when things don't go as planned at a fire or rescue."

"So what do you do about it?"

"Try to do better the next time and the time after that and so on. I once had a very wise instructor who was asked about the percentages of success administering CPR. Know what she said?"

Sara silently shook her head.

"She said, 'It's not up to you to make it work. Your job is to do exactly what you've been trained for, to the best of your ability, and leave the results up to God.'"

"She said that? Right in class?"

"Yes. And I still remember her words to this day. She was right on. We are expected to do the best with what we know in any circumstance. That's it. Vicki made a judgment call and it was the wrong one. Her loss is not on your shoulders. She died because she made the wrong decision instead of using the good sense God gave her."

"She was a believer. A Christian."

"Which means that you and I are promised we'll see her again one day, but that's not the same as believing the Lord was going to bail her out if and when she acted foolishly."

Sara got his message, she truly did, although she didn't like hearing it put quite that way. "Are you trying to comfort me or giving me a lecture about not taking chances?"

"A little of both." He started her car and backed out of the parking place. "I'm going to take you to the drive-in just up the highway so we can order and eat sitting right where we are."

"Fine. I don't care."

"No rules against fries or catsup in your car?"

She huffed softly as she glanced over at him. "Was there ever?"

"Just checking."

The hint of a smile quirked one corner of his mouth and she could tell he was doing his best to lift her spirits. That was Adam all over. He not only cared that she was physically safe; he showed concern for her mood, as well.

Sara appreciated his efforts enough to try to respond the way she knew he wanted her to. She wrestled down her depression and worked up a smile. Just for him. Just for her last best friend in the world.

"We can use the bags the food comes in to collect our trash," she said. "I won't object to eating in here unless you start a food fight."

"Have I ever—"

She interrupted with a firm, "Yes."

"That was a long time ago. I was a dumb kid."

Sighing, Sara felt her smile spreading as she envisioned their youth and the fun they'd shared. "You were never a dumb anything, Adam. You may have been ornery and troublesome and the biggest joker in town but you were always intelligent."

He sobered. "I made my share of mistakes."

"Yeah. We all did."

Their conversation was suspended as Adam wheeled in the fast-food-restaurant driveway and pulled into one of the angled dining spaces. Sara was far more interested in hearing him enumerate his mistakes than she was in eating. To her dismay, he dropped the subject and she lost her opportunity to probe without making a big deal of it. Had he been thinking about his choice to leave town when she was eighteen? Did he consider that a serious error? Perhaps. But it was just as likely that he was thinking he should have stayed and married Vicki. After all, she'd been the one who threw herself at him, and what virile young man wouldn't have been thrilled to be the object of such tangible affection?

Sara relaxed in the front seat and let Adam order for her. It was heartwarming to hear that he remembered her favorites. She could just as easily have predicted what he would order, except for the drink. Soda had been replaced by plain ice tea.

Although her head was laid back, her eyes closed, she could feel his closeness, revel in his presence beside her. It wasn't a surprise when he took her hand. She wove her fingers between his and held tight. "Being here like this takes me back. You?"

"Yes." The low rumble of his voice touched every nerve in her body.

A surprising sense of rightness and peace surged through her, coming to rest in her wounded heart. This was one of those precious moments that were all too rare and therefore totally memorable.

A carload of teens, including Adam and Sara, used to come to this drive-in after school and following Friday night football games to share snacks and playfully tease each other rather than settle down in specific couples. Or so it had seemed at the time.

In retrospect, Sara recalled the way her cousin had flirted with all the boys and sometimes focused her romantic interest on one of them for a short while. Adam had been slightly older, Vicki a little younger, so he had treated her as if he were her big brother most of the time.

Most, but not all, Sara reminded herself. By the time Vicki turned eighteen he was already a marine. Who knows what might have happened if he'd stayed in Paradise? Might he have fallen for Vicki all the way and married her?

Adam had seemed a bit frazzled when Vicki had thrown her arms around his neck and planted a kiss on his lips in parting. And his gaze had darted to her, Sara, rather than concentrating on that embarrassing action. For the first time, it occurred to Sara that he might have been avoiding her cousin, rather than her. Was that possible? Had he been silently pleading for understanding? For rescue? For a change of partners that Sara had not been prepared to provide? If so, was it too late to rectify her error of omission?

She opened her eyes as she gave his hand a squeeze and released it, adding a gentle smile to soften the parting. Adam looked a little confused by her mellower mood. Well, he wasn't the only one. Introspection usually brought increased emotional upheaval. This time, however, those thoughts had soothed her spirit.

"I think I am getting hungry," she said brightly. "I'm glad you insisted on lunch."

He was staring at her as if she'd climbed out the window and begun clogging like a folk dancer on the hood of the car. Imagining herself doing that widened her smile.

His brow furrowed. "What's so funny?"

"I am," Sara easily admitted. "It's just occurred to me

that I may have misinterpreted the motives behind some things that had upset me in the past."

"Do I figure in this epiphany of yours?"

Her smile twisted wryly. "Maybe."

"Care to share?"

"Nope. Not yet." *And perhaps never*, Sara added to herself. First, she'd have to decide if she was correct. Then she'd need to see if Adam still considered her special. In the meantime, there was his penchant for acting as her guardian, which was not only advantageous but gave her a reason to stay close to him, to hopefully work through their problems. Events that had initially seemed senseless were beginning to strike her as having a dual purpose. That conclusion fit with her pastor's teaching. Just because something was terrible on the one hand, didn't mean the Lord couldn't ultimately use it for the good of His followers. His children.

The arrival of their food was a welcome distraction. Adam passed it to her so he could pay the carhop. By the time their bill was settled, Sara was nearly ready to eat. Holding her burger she took a moment to pray silently over it. When Adam added his own "Amen," she was both surprised and happy. They had so much in common it was scary. And thrilling. They were no longer kids, no longer seeking the path to becoming the balanced adults they were meant to be. They had arrived. Together.

Sara was smiling when she gazed over at Adam, expecting him to mirror her feeling of camaraderie. Instead, he was ignoring her and peering into the rearview mirror.

She sobered, tensing. "What is it? What do you see?"

"Nothing. Eat."

"Don't start that again, please. The best way for you to protect me is to explain what you're doing and seeing, not keep me in the dark so I won't be scared. Believe me, I'm a lot safer when I'm on edge."

Adam nodded. "You're right. Sorry. I'm not positive but I may have spotted the same guy I caught watching you in the store."

"You didn't tell me about that, either."

"Yes, I did. But he left just as I pointed him out to you. He was big and tattooed, maybe like you saw on the drive-by shooter, although that's no proof this guy was going to cause problems. What I noticed was the way he stood. The way he kept staring at you. And the fact that I didn't see him pushing a shopping cart like everybody else."

Sara swiveled as far as she could to check the area behind her car. "Where is he?"

"Gone again," Adam said. "That's another reason I didn't make a big deal out of it. I thought I caught a glimpse of him as he drove by. I could have been mistaken."

"Do you think you were?" She took a long pull on her straw so the ice tea would help clear her tightening throat.

When Adam said, "No," that and the cold drink brought a shiver that shook her from head to toe.

Rewrapping and passing her the uneaten portion of his lunch, Adam started the car. "We're leaving. Hang on." Sara surprised him by complying without argument. *Good.* She was learning to trust his judgment enough to make his job easier. Now all he had to do was figure out who was after her and stop them.

"Where are we going?"

"Back to the ranch?"

"I'd rather not."

Since he'd anticipated a more forceful refusal he took her comment in stride. "Okay, then where?"

"How about the fire station? It's close and we can go inside to eat before the food gets cold."

And set me up to be teased mercilessly, Adam thought. Was he ready to cope with his coworker's taunts? Everybody knew that he and Sara were old friends but lately their relationship felt different to him. More personal. Even romantic. Yes, it was simply a quick lunch, yet there was a subtle element to their being together that convinced him others would also sense a change.

Did Sara feel it, too? Adam wondered. Maybe she did, maybe she didn't. He could ask her, of course. When the timing was right. For the present he figured he'd be doing well to stay on her good side and convince her to do things his way most of the time.

She was staring at him as he drove. "Well?"

"Yeah, sure. We can eat in the break room or the kitchen. The guys won't care."

"How about you? Will you care, Adam?"

"I don't know what you're getting at."

A slight lift of her shoulders looked like a shrug. "Don't you? Then why do I have the impression you don't want to take me with you to the station? We're there at the same time for calls and for weekly training. How is this any different?"

Ah, here was his opportunity. Should he take advantage of it? As a prelude, he chuckled and shook his head. "I feel like I'm tiptoeing through a minefield, Sara."

"Why? What did I do?"

"Nothing. Everything. I'd been wondering if you were beginning to view our time together as a little more than the meeting of two old friends."

"If I say I am, then what?"

"Then I'd have to admit that I am, too." Adam smiled

over at her briefly as he drove. "Of course, if you say no, then I'll deny that I ever asked."

"How about if I plead the Fifth?"

"I don't think that counts unless you're under oath in a court of law."

"Oh."

He noticed a reddening of her cheeks and suspected she might be having as much trouble dealing with a change in their status as he was. Unfortunately, they had arrived at the fire station and their time for private conversation was at an end.

Adam got out, circled to open her car door and helped her carry their food. Clay and a new hire named Nate were outdoors polishing one of the engines and joking with each other. They stopped as soon as they noticed the new arrivals.

"We're going to go have lunch in the break room," Adam announced as they passed, preempting any queries.

Nate gave a subdued nod. Clay, however, hooted the way a fan would if his favorite team scored a homerun. "Woo-hoo! You go, Captain."

Adam knew his neck and face were too hot to have maintained his normal complexion so he hurried ahead to hold the interior door for Sara. "That's what I was afraid of."

"What? That they'd notice we're together? It's not terribly unusual." The expression she presented when she put down her drink cup and turned to look at him seemed to suggest a hint of unrest as well as a tinge of amusement.

"It's also not funny, Sara."

"Oh, I don't know. Most of the men and women who work here have known us since we were in high school, or before. They probably figured out years ago that I had a crush on you."

"No way."

"Oh no? Why do you think I begged you to stay in Paradise instead of enlisting?"

"You were worried about me."

"Yes. And much more. But I could tell you only had eyes for my cousin so I never told you how I felt."

"Unbelievable."

"Not to me." She slid into a chair at the table and proceeded to redistribute their lunch. "Now, are you going to stand there looking stunned and drawing attention to yourself, or are you going to sit down and eat?"

Adam sat. She was right. He was somewhat stunned. He was also confused. What had given her the notion that he'd preferred Vicki? At the time he'd left town he hadn't had romantic notions about any women; he'd simply wanted to escape from the small town he'd thought was stifling him. Boy, had he been wrong. There was nothing like facing death in a foreign country to convince a guy he belonged back on home turf.

And the letters the cousins had written to him hadn't given him a clue. They'd both been chatty and friendly and promised prayer for his well-being. Granted, he hadn't been good about writing back but that was because he didn't want to share the ravages of combat, not because he devalued their friendship.

Well, at least he now had his answer. Sara did care for him, or at least she once had. There was no reason to assume she'd changed her mind. If she had, she wouldn't have admitted a romantic crush, would she?

In retrospect, Adam could see as clearly as a reflection in the polished chrome of the engines. Her affection had been low-key while Vicki had thrown herself into his arms for a goodbye kiss. Yet it was Sara who had had tears in her eyes as they'd waved goodbye to him.

And it was Sara whose life was now in his hands. One thing was certain. His military training and experience were going to be of the most value in protecting her. The very same training she had begged him to avoid.

Talk about divine providence!

FOURTEEN

It was all Sara could do to swallow nibbles of her hamburger. Had it really taken threats to her life to wake up Adam? Apparently. She knew she should be thankful but wished he could have realized how she felt via less painful means.

She was able to catch snatches of muted conversations in the background as on-duty firefighters went about their daily assignments. As the main topic of their conversation, she wished the others had more chores to distract them but it was what it was. Chief Ellis had often observed that members of the department who had trained hard and signed up to save lives had to be kept busy all the time or they'd get into more trouble than a half-grown litter of pups.

In a way, she was the same. When she wasn't at work or acting as a volunteer EMT she had way too much time to think. To fret. And to argue with herself about everything, as she was doing right now.

She peered over the edge of her large cup, sized up Adam and decided he was doing his best to ignore her. *Say something. No, don't. Yes. Speak up. Finish what you started in the car and get it all out in the open.*

And then what? she asked herself. If she pushed him,

pressed for answers and ended up being wrong about what he'd confess, her heart and her life would be in worse turmoil than they already were. There was only one sensible course of action. She had to let it go. At least for the present.

Reverting to the comfortable role of caregiver, she gathered up their sandwich wrappers, wiped the table with a spare napkin, deposited it all in the trash and dusted her palms together. "Okay. Let's roll."

Adam was finishing his ice tea. "Where are we going?"

"Hunting. I know there must be photos of the members of the gang Rigo was part of. If the sheriff or police don't already have them I know they can get them by email. You did get a good look at the guy in the store, right?"

"Yes. I studied him for as long as possible."

"Wonderful."

Adam rose slowly, tossed away his empty cup and studied her. "You sure change moods fast."

"It's a coping skill," Sara replied. "I may feel terrible about something, like losing a patient on my shift no matter how hard I've worked to save him, but I'm no good to all my other patients if I brood. The same thing is true of being hurt by Helen Babcock. It was traumatic, sure, but dwelling on how bad she made me feel gets me nowhere."

"Astute. Also hard to do. Did you learn that in nursing school?"

"Not directly. I think it developed as I matured in my faith. First, I remind myself God loves me. Then I think about all the trials He's brought me through. Then I pray and do my best to release whatever is bothering me to keep it from eating away at my peace. And then I try to find a way to act in a positive manner to further the healing process. That usually works pretty well—when I remember to do it."

"You really think looking at mug shots is going to help the investigation?"

"Can't hurt. Might help."

"Okay. I'm game. Let's go."

He shooed her out the door, making her laugh softly. "Easy, cowboy. I'm not one of your calves. You don't have to herd me."

"Just trying to avoid extra teasing."

Sara laughed more. "It's way too late for that and you know it. I really am sorry. When I suggested eating at the station I never thought about starting new rumors."

"Don't sweat it. In a town like Paradise it was only a matter of time before somebody noticed how much we've been together lately."

"Yes, but you always say it's because you're protecting me from the bad guys."

"I am." He gestured past the car and said, "Shall we walk again? It's not far."

"And a lovely spring day, besides." She rubbed her upper arms. "I wish I'd thought to bring a jacket."

"Want mine?"

"No, thanks. We won't be outside long and it's warmer in the sun." Falling into step with Adam she managed to keep up by adding an extra step for every three of his. "I hope you'll be able to recognize somebody in the gang pictures."

He abruptly stopped walking. Grabbed her arm to halt her forward momentum. Pulled her closer to his side and leaned to whisper, "I know I will. I can see him right now."

"Where?" Her head began to swivel. Adam's hands cupped her cheeks, held her still. "Don't look. Don't react. We can't turn back to the fire station or he'll know we've spotted and recognized him."

"But—"

"Trust me, honey," Adam whispered. "I've got this."

Sara's lips parted. Her breath was ragged, her heart racing. She wanted desperately to look at the man Adam thought posed a danger but he was preventing it.

"Do you kiss with your eyes closed?" he asked.

That was the last question she'd expected. "Why?"

"If you do, keep them open this time and you'll see."

With that, he drew her into his arms, turned her slightly and gave her the most amazing kiss she'd ever experienced. It was so awesome she forgot his instructions. Her lids lowered slightly, fluttering.

Adam eased off only enough to say, "Look," then continued to kiss her. Her brain argued against it, blaming Adam's demonstration of his kissing on his need to show her the stranger he thought was a danger. At this point she didn't really care. Not while he continued to kiss her.

It was a monumental struggle to focus on the figure in the distance rather than on Adam but she finally managed. The man was seated on one of the benches arranged on the lawn bordering the courthouse. He was glaring at her and Adam.

Sara had already been short of breath because of being kissed. Now, she felt suffocated.

She knew exactly who her nemesis was!

With a strangled gasp she pushed at Adam's shoulders and spoke softly into his ear. "Hector. Hector Alvarez."

"You know him." It wasn't a question.

"Yes."

Feeling her start to sway, Adam supported her as he whispered, "I'm going to turn you back the right way now and we're going to keep walking. Understand?"

"Uh-huh."

He knew better than to let go of her when she was wobbling like a newborn calf. "That's it, honey. One foot after the other. We're almost there."

"Is he following us?"

"I don't think so. I caught a glimpse of his reflection when we passed a window and he wasn't moving."

"Good."

"Just keep going," Adam said. "Don't let on that he's rattled you."

"Excuse me?"

Adam clarified. "It's better if he thinks you're in control."

"I am in control."

He knew better than to laugh or challenge her. "Okay. Whatever you say. He probably didn't notice how unsteady you were for a minute there."

Sara kept moving ahead but he could feel her spine stiffening, her body language practically shouting indignation. He shooed her through the door to the police station before he asked, "What's wrong with you?"

"Me? Nothing."

"Could have fooled me." When he saw her roll her eyes and arch her eyebrows in a clear display of disgust he was flabbergasted. "Why are you acting so grumpy? We'll get the cops to pick him up and your troubles will be over."

"Over? Oh, sure. I suppose, in spite of the way you kissed me just now, you expect me to forget all about it."

"Is that what's got your feathers ruffled? I was trying to provide a rational way for you to get a glimpse of the guy without letting you turn around and stare at him. It was a brilliant idea. He never caught on."

"Brilliant," she grumbled as she made her way to the dispatcher to report their sighting.

Standing behind Sara for moral support and listening

to her explanation regarding her stalker, Adam kept one eye on the door, just in case. For the present he was planning to feign cluelessness and let her assume she hadn't knocked his socks off when she'd kissed him back. Talk about astounding! That experience was far more than a simple kiss. It was a tender joining of their spirits with undertones of unspoken promise.

He was no naïve kid. He'd been kissed before. But this time he'd been so deeply moved, he'd hardly been able to keep his own balance, let alone steady Sara. She'd made his head swim, his nerves tingle and his thoughts take flight. That reaction might have been fine under different circumstances but it could be deadly when he needed to be 100 percent on guard.

Meaning, he'd better not give in and kiss her again until he was certain her troubles were over. Hopefully, when this gang member was arrested and questioned, they'd learn enough to finish the case and put everyone's fears to rest. Then he'd somehow have to make her believe that he'd had a good enough reason to kiss her when he did without admitting he'd nearly drowned in the ensuing flood of emotions.

Adam clenched his fists. One thing was certain. He had made a mistake when he'd used a kiss as the means to keep her out of danger. A big, big mistake. Probably one of the biggest of his adult life.

"Cecelia says we can watch the arrest from in here," Sara told Adam. She preceded him to the plate-glass window facing the street. There was a latticework of wrought iron protecting the exterior from anyone who might want illegal access to the offices and files, not to mention the holding cells in the rear.

He cupped her shoulders from behind. "Don't get too close to the glass, just in case he can see in."

"I'm not going to miss this. Not for anything."

"Fair enough. I guess you're entitled."

Officers appeared on the far side of the courthouse lawn and began to spread out behind the burly stalker. He fidgeted, making Sara afraid he might sense his own peril and perhaps turn around. If he saw his captors coming she knew he'd make a run for it. Above all, he must not escape. She had to know whether or not Vicki had been murdered.

Hector shifted his position, clearly uneasy. Sara ducked out from under Adam's hands and hurried to the main entrance, determined to be in position to make her move, if necessary, before anyone had a chance to intervene.

I am not being foolish, she insisted. *I can peek out the door and distract Hector if he starts to leave.* As far as she was concerned, her impromptu plan was perfect as well as being relatively safe.

Her fingers closed on the handle. Ignoring everything else she leaned to push the door open a crack.

Behind her, Adam shouted, "No!"

Already on edge, Sara let out a staccato yip. That caused the startled gang member to jump to his feet and bolt, apparently not even noticing her. For a huge man he moved well. Too well.

The deputies across the lawn began to pursue him on foot shouting, "Stop! Police!" A patrol car's lights and siren came on as the unmarked car burned rubber and paralleled the courthouse.

All that mayhem turbocharged Hector's flight. He was headed for the narrow alley between the police and fire stations. If he reached it and got through before the officers overtook him, Sara knew he'd have access to the firefighters and their vehicles. It didn't take a criminologist to figure he was armed and dangerous.

Adam burst out past her, letting the door swing free. His trajectory was obviously meant to intercept the fleeing man but she could tell he was going to be late. Then he'd probably follow Hector into the alley and become a sitting duck. Sara didn't have time to reason. She simply acted.

Stepping out onto the sidewalk and shading her eyes from bright sunlight with one hand, she waved the other in the air. "Hey! Hector! Over here."

Hearing his name must have broken through his fight-or-flight reaction because he skidded to a stop, turned and stared at her. That was exactly the result she'd hoped for. The cops were closing on him from the rear, the patrol car was rounding the final corner in the square, and Adam was only a dozen heartbeats from success.

Time seemed to drag, suspended for the moments while Sara faced her stalker. She was already panting. When he began to leer at her she lost all capacity to breathe. Frozen in place on the sidewalk, she saw him pull a shiny object from his belt!

His arm came up, pointing a pistol straight at her. His other hand clasped the first. He widened his stance.

Run! her mind screamed. *Run!*

Muscles tight, she crouched and pivoted. Leaned away. Felt as if she were trying to swim through a vat of molasses.

If she'd had breath to spare she'd have screamed. Instead, she staggered forward in a desperate attempt to outrun a bullet. There was no time for thought, no time to chastise herself. And no way to go back and make different choices. All she did have time for was a single word prayer, "Jesus!"

The toe of her shoe caught in a tiny crack on the sidewalk. She lost her balance. Surged forward and landed on her hands and knees on the concrete. Momentum continued to push her forward. Her arms folded at the elbows, planting her chin on the ground with a whack that jarred her teeth.

At that same instant Hector fired.

The pain in Sara's jaw convinced her she'd been shot. Had she saved everybody else? She certainly hoped so. If Adam was all right he'd be standing in line behind the police chief, ready to give her a lecture, but she didn't care. As long as she was the only casualty and the others had captured Hector, she had accomplished her purpose.

Random thoughts swam in and out of her consciousness, most of them self-deprecating. Where had such idiotic bravado come from? As a kid she'd climbed trees, gone canoeing or jumped bikes with her friends, but she'd thought she had outgrown such risky behavior. So why had she hollered to distract a gunman when she'd have been safe if she'd kept quiet?

Because I think this is all my fault? Sara asked herself. *Do I?* That was the most logical excuse she could come up with and even that one made less sense than she'd have liked.

"Who cares?" she muttered, rolling onto her back. Her jaw hurt, her head was throbbing, her knees smarted and her elbows and palms were issuing their own complaints.

A din surrounded her. Men were shouting. Car engines were racing. The bright sun blinded her, made her eyes sting and water.

She started to sit up. Flashes of colored lights burst at the edges of her field of vision. Was she falling? Floating? Did she care? Nope. Finally she'd found peace and quiet and she intended to lie there and enjoy it.

FIFTEEN

Adam had been in midair, diving for the gunman's knees, when the pistol fired. He felt the bullet whiz past his left ear and instinctively threw himself the opposite way. If Sara had stayed where he'd last seen her she was the intended target!

Recovering and pivoting in a crouch, he had nanoseconds to see for himself. She was down! His heart clenched as if caught in the grip of a giant's fist. Peripheral vision warned too late that the gun was swinging his way. Hard steel slammed into the side of his head.

Stunned, Adam rolled away and landed on all fours, finding his feet and charging at Hector with a gut-wrenching roar that embodied all of Sara's pain as well as his own. This was a battle unlike any he'd fought before. More than honor and duty drove him. This man had hurt his Sara. He deserved the worst punishment possible.

Adam dove straight into Hector's broad chest, knocked him backward, wrestled away the gun and began to drive punches at his face until he was pulled off by law enforcement officers.

They held him firm while he struggled. "Let me go! He shot Sara."

"No, he didn't," one of them shouted. "She just fell."

"He shot her. I saw!"

It took two burly deputies to hold him back while others tended to Hector, quickly cuffing him and searching him for additional weapons. The gun was bagged as evidence.

Adam saw a crowd gathering on the sidewalk across the street. *Sara!* He wrenched loose and took off running, calling, "Sara!" over and over. Ragged breaths tore from him as his heart and mind struggled to come to grips with what he saw.

Paramedics from the nearby fire station cleared the area just as Adam burst through the line of onlookers. He blinked, unbelieving. She was moving! Sara was alive! Not only that, she almost looked pleased with herself.

Angst turned to anger, fondness to fury. He dropped to his knees beside her. "I thought you were shot."

"So did I, for a second."

Adam was still gasping. "How—how did he miss?"

"I tripped. I think God pushed me out of the way."

Levering himself to his feet he stepped back to give the medics room to conduct their patient assessment. He was fuming. His gut was tied in a knot and his heart about to pound out of his chest. How was it possible to be so glad to see her and yet feel so angry he wanted to yell at the top of his lungs?

This was the wrong time to express himself but somebody had to do something to get her to start thinking before she acted.

The instant she looked up at him and asked, "Did they get him? Did they arrest Hector?" Adam lost it.

"Do you have any idea how crazy it was to show yourself like that? You put everybody else in danger when your Texas buddy could have been captured without violence."

Sara didn't seem to be listening. She started to get to

her feet despite the medics' warnings to stay still. Adam grasped her upper arms to steady her.

She struggled. "Let me go. I have to see."

Practically nose to nose, Adam stared her down. "They got him, okay. No thanks to you."

"You're mad at me?"

"Oh, yeah. Good and mad."

"Why?"

Was she serious? Words were totally insufficient and Adam knew the ones he might choose at that moment were unacceptable, so he struggled to tame his temper.

Sara tilted her head. "Your ear is bleeding. What happened?"

Touching the injury and seeing red on his fingertips reminded him he'd felt a bullet's graze. He huffed. "I got hurt trying to take care of you again. You'd think I'd have better sense by this time." That got her full attention.

Her expression began with astonishment, passed through guilt and ended apologetic, contrite and teary-eyed. "Oh, Adam, I'm so sorry. I was just trying to keep Hector from getting away. You have to understand that."

Seeing her new awareness helped him calm down enough to accompany her and the medics to the nearby ambulance so they could both be treated.

"Aren't you going to say anything?" Sara asked.

Meeting her misty gaze he shook his head. "Not if you expect me to tell you I'm happy you risked your life."

One of the ambulance attendants handed her a cool, damp cloth and Sara pressed it to her injured chin. Smiling was painful but that wasn't what kept her somber. Watching the paramedic bandaging Adam's ear hurt her more than it did him. Contrite, she finally made eye contact with him. "You said they arrested Hector, right?"

"Yes."

"Good. Maybe this is the end of it."

"Did you really trip over nothing? That sidewalk looks smooth."

"I know. But I managed to stumble at the right time so don't knock it."

Adam raised his hands. "Hey, I'm good with whatever saved you. If God gave you a shove, like you said, it's fine with me."

"That's the first thing that popped into my head. I know it sounds silly."

"Not to me." He froze as she reached up and touched the small bandage on his left ear.

"What happened?"

"It's just a scratch."

"Scratches don't leave the groove I saw. Bullets do."

"Does it matter, Sara? We're both relatively sound and Hector is in jail. Life is good. Okay?"

"Okay." She knew he was right about counting blessings. Still, there were loose ends to tie up. "I want to go back to the police station so we'll know as soon as he talks."

"Do you really think he will? He's in deep trouble and he knows it. If I were him I'd keep my mouth shut and ask for a lawyer."

Sighing, she tried to hide her disappointment. "I suppose you're right. This has been such a trying day I hardly know what to do with myself."

"I can tell. So, what'll it be? Your place or mine?"

"Very funny."

"But a sensible question. Are you ready to move into the house behind the co-op or would you rather go back to the ranch with me?"

Shrugging, she said, "I wish I knew what was best."

"Tell you what." He looped an arm lightly around her shoulders. "Since we aren't sure if the cops are through inspecting your new place and I have work to do out at the ranch, why don't you follow me home for one more night and start fresh in the morning?"

"And use my own car? I see what you mean. If I drive myself I'll be able to go straight to the hospital to go over my schedule with my supervisor. She's probably tearing her hair out wondering if I'll show up for my shift tomorrow evening."

Sara noted a sobering of Adam's expression. "Are you sure you want to do that? I mean, we're not positive your problems are over yet."

"I'm sure enough," she countered. "If Hector talks, fine. If he doesn't, there's not a thing I can do about it. I may as well go on with my everyday life and make the best of it." She managed a demure smile, hoping it would lift his mood. "Besides, we have guards at the hospital and closed-circuit cameras in all the hallways. Nobody is going to try anything there."

"Maybe you could borrow a protective vest from the police."

"Oh, sure. That would inspire a lot of confidence from my patients." She rolled her eyes at him. "And don't bother to try convincing me I need to be armed. It's not allowed where I work."

"You do have a concealed-carry permit, right?"

"Only because my dad insisted. I see no reason to run around like a posse of one when we have such great law enforcement people in Paradise." Another sigh. "Besides, I obviously don't know how to tell bad guys from good guys."

It was not flattering to her ego when Adam nodded sagely and said, "You're right about that."

* * *

Adam never took his eyes off Sara's car as he followed her out to his ranch. She was driving slowly, cautiously, so much so that his nerves were on edge more than ever. He smacked the steering wheel with an open hand.

"What am I going to do with you, Sara?" he asked the empty air. That question had no perfect answer. Since he had foolishly kissed her, his emotions were in such a turmoil he hardly knew his own name, let alone what plans he should be making in regard to the woman who was driving him crazy.

Did she have feelings for him? That answer came from the sweet memory of her kissing him so ardently. So now what? Pursue her? Give her time to grieve the loss of Vicki so he'd be sure she wasn't just looking for solace? Above all, Adam didn't want to ruin a possible good thing by being too pushy. This Sara wasn't the same light-hearted young woman he'd had innocent fun with when they were teens. This Sara was strong. Decisive.

His jaw clenched as he pictured the scene on the court-house lawn and in front of the police station. This Sara was also too brave, too quick to jump in without testing the depth of the proverbial ocean—and in her case the water was filled with hungry sharks.

By the time their vehicles reached Kane Ranch, Adam had mentally explored every possibility and rejected them all. Until they had more information on Sara's attacker or attackers there was no way to logically plan an offense. Playing defense was his only option and he wasn't thrilled.

She parked in front of the main house and Adam pulled close behind her, noting the familiar pillowcase she'd been using as luggage. "I forgot you never unpacked."

"Never had the time or opportunity," she replied.

"Right. I took the liberty of asking Chief Magill to keep an eye on your new place."

"You didn't have to do that."

Adam couldn't tell whether or not she was upset so he dropped the subject. As far as he was concerned, he'd do and say whatever he deemed necessary in order to safeguard Sara, even if that made her mad.

He gestured toward the front door. "I suggest we go in and crash. I don't know about you but I've had it."

He couldn't miss her cynical expression and pointed glance at his injured ear. "I'll want to check that bandage."

"The paramedics know what they're doing."

"Yes, but what's the use of having a nurse in residence if you don't use her? I worry about infection."

"My tetanus shots are up to date," Adam said with a slight smile. "I'll be fine."

She preceded him onto the porch, insisting she could tote her own makeshift baggage. "I know you'll be okay because I intend to see to it."

"Did anybody ever tell you you're stubborn as a mule?"

"Takes one to know one."

He laughed. "You've got that right, lady. Ask my brothers."

"I expected to find them home." Sara hesitated on her way to the kitchen. "Where is everybody?"

"A ranch takes lots of work. We don't just fence in a herd of cattle and let them graze. They have to be cared for. So do the horses and chickens, not to mention a wife and children, in Carter's case."

"Twins must be hard on Missy," Sara remarked, continuing into the kitchen after plopping her bag of clothing on the sofa.

"Beats me. I plan to start acting like an uncle when

they get old enough to walk and talk. Right now they kinda scare me."

"I know what you mean." She scooted onto a stool and propped her elbows on the kitchen bar. "I never babysat like Vicki did. She was the one who was good with toddlers."

Keeping his back to her on purpose, Adam opened the refrigerator and took inventory. "I suppose you'd learn if you had kids of your own. Want a cold soda?"

He paused, waiting for her to either make a joke about children or take him seriously. She did neither. When he straightened and turned to face her, she looked pale. At least he thought she did. When it came to Sara Southerland he may as well be a stranger facing some kind of beautiful alien and trying to make sense of a foreign language.

Putting a can of soda on the bar in front of her he said, "Here you go. Want a snack, too?"

"I'm not hungry."

"You didn't have a big lunch. Let me get you something now." He struggled to sound casual. "You know you need fuel to make your brain work well. We both have to be at the top of our game."

"That's what this is, isn't it? A game. A cruel, evil game that somebody is playing with me—and I don't even know the rules."

"Maybe not, but you and I have our faith." He took one of her hands across the narrow breakfast bar. "I admit I wasn't as good at trusting the Lord as I should have been when I was in tough situations overseas, but I'm starting to see that He's with us, with you, here in Paradise."

"It doesn't feel like it right now."

"That doesn't mean it isn't true, Sara. God may have rescued you time after time when you were oblivious to

His actions on your behalf. Think about it. You gave Him credit for tripping so the bullet missed you."

She sighed heavily. "You're right. And I'm not grateful enough, am I?"

As soon as Adam covered her hand with his free one, she mirrored him by adding hers. There was moisture glistening in her sky blue eyes when she raised them to meet his darker gaze. His imagination soared as he recognized concern and perhaps more. They would talk about their burgeoning feelings soon. He would see to it.

And now? Now there were logistics to put in place. Defense plans to make. Arrangements to explain to his brothers so they wouldn't put themselves in danger if—when—someone else came after Sara.

Was he wrong to plan for the worst? *No*, Adam decided easily. The soldier who got lax about his duty became a soft target. And the rancher who didn't tag or brand his cattle was asking to have his herd rustled.

What about the man who failed to confess his feelings for a woman and then lost her? he added. Adam tightened his grip, noting that Sara squeezed back. "I'm sorry I left you all those years ago," he said gently. "We were young, maybe too young, but I should have given you a chance to explain yourself to me."

She began to smile, eyes glistening. "I was really shy back then, Adam. I probably would have run from you if you'd gotten too serious. Everything is a lot clearer in retrospect."

"It is, isn't it?" He cleared his throat. "If I had any doubts left, they disappeared when I thought you'd been shot."

"Doubts?"

As he watched her smile widen he sensed that she

was enjoying his struggle. "About you and me. Us. As a couple. Don't tell me you haven't felt something, too."

"Well…"

Just then a door slammed and Kurt burst into the kitchen. "Bro! I saw your truck but wasn't sure whose car that was. Hey, Sara. Welcome back."

Adam had instinctively jumped at the sight of his brother. So had Sara. They were no longer holding hands. When he reached to grab hers again, she eased away. The mood was gone, the moment of truth postponed, although there was little doubt in Adam's heart and mind that they shared an emotional bond.

Kurt took a cold soda out of the refrigerator and popped the top, offering it to Sara. She motioned to the one she already had so he took a deep drink himself. "Suit yourself. *Mi casa es su casa*, as they say."

"Since when do you speak Spanish?" Adam asked.

His younger brother shrugged. "Guess it was just on my mind after all the fun I heard you had in town this afternoon."

"Whatever you heard it was probably exaggerated."

"Probably. You might want to give the cops a call, though. Deputy Elmer was looking for you earlier."

"He was? What for?" Rising, Adam circled the end of the breakfast bar and stopped to stand next to Sara because he didn't like the sudden seriousness he was sensing in Kurt.

"Something about somebody vandalizing her apartment."

"That's old news," Sara said, sounding relieved.

"Uh-uh. Not the paint. This is something new. Elmer was cruising by the co-op and spotted a guy coming out of a place behind their office. He knew Sara was planning to move there so he stopped and checked."

Adam heard her breath hitch and slipped his arm around her shoulders. "And?"

"And it was wrecked inside. Busted up with a sledge-hammer, they think."

SIXTEEN

Sara sipped at her soda to stall until Kurt left. When they were alone again, Adam started to give her instructions about staying out of sight and she balked.

"Why should vandalism keep me from going to work?"

"Because," Adam said.

"Because?" She was acting braver than she felt, yet that was the only course her pride would allow. Processing the most recent information had made her tremble inside, sure, but that didn't mean she was going to hide from life.

"For one thing, Hector was in jail," Adam said.

"Maybe he did the damage earlier."

Adam heaved a sigh. "Yeah, maybe. And maybe there's somebody else around who has a score to settle with you. Did you think of that?"

"Of course I did. As soon as they convince Hector to talk we'll know. In the meantime, the hospital needs me. And I need wages." Seeing his distress she mellowed a little. "Look. If you're off tomorrow and you want to escort me to work, fine. I'll go along with that. But I am going."

"You checked with your supervisor already?"

"Yes. Gloria texted me and I agreed to the afternoon shift in ER. They're short staffed."

Varying emotions flashed across his face so rapidly she wasn't sure what she was seeing. Finally, he nodded. "Okay. Have it your way. Do you promise to stay in the house now while I go do my chores?"

"Why don't I come along and help you?" Sara was astonished when Adam shook his head.

"Not a good idea. You'll be safer inside. I'm going to saddle up and run the fences."

"Can I at least go to the barn with you? I spotted some darling kittens the other day."

"They're feral barn cats. They're liable to take your arm off if you try to pet them."

"They didn't run away when I saw them before. One almost let me touch it. They know I love them."

"What you need is a big, protective dog, not a little cat. As soon as the police say it's safe for you to move back to town we'll work on that."

"Now you're picking out my pets, too?"

"Oh, for crying out loud, Sara. I'm trying to help you here. I care about you, okay?" He muttered something else to himself.

"What did you say? I didn't catch that."

When he made a face and said, "You weren't supposed to," he sounded so much like his old self she almost giggled.

Sara's dreams that night were centered around a handsome cowboy on a magnificent steed who kept racing to her rescue and scooping her up to ride with him into the sunset. Waking up and leaving that perfect hero behind was a downer.

Nevertheless, she was excited about going back to work. Her career helped define her, and although maturity had made her self-sufficient to the nth degree, there was still a place in her heart that longed for that special cowboy. She hadn't needed to see the face in her dreams to know exactly who he was.

As promised, she encouraged Adam to follow her to town. Thankfully, he didn't insist on walking her into the hospital the way a parent escorted a recalcitrant child to class. She gave him a wave as she entered through the glass ER doors and paused until she saw him drive off.

Then she turned and became the capable nurse she knew she was. Between reassuring her coworkers that she was okay and tending to a heavy patient load, time passed swiftly. This was where she was in her element, where she felt the most useful and skilled. By evening, a good weariness gave her peace and she realized she'd stayed too busy to fret much about her personal problems.

A middle-aged nurse in blue scrubs caught up to her in the hallway. "Did you hear?"

Sara frowned. "Hear what?"

"There's been a terrible wreck out on the highway between here and Mountain Grove."

Sara's heart was already beginning to speed up. If there was a bad accident that close, the Paradise Fire Department had probably been dispatched.

"I heard it on the scanner," the nurse said, pointing to their break room. "Are you going?"

"Not if they're bringing victims to us."

"I doubt it," her coworker said. "The ambulance was dispatched from Koshkonong."

"In that case I'll grab my purse and notify Gloria that I'm leaving. ER is quiet anyway."

Sara was in her car, racing in the direction of the reported accident, before she remembered that Adam was supposed to follow her back to his ranch since her new home had not yet been repaired after the latest vandalism.

That would have bothered her more if she didn't assume that he'd be doing exactly what she was doing, responding to the call in his private vehicle. That was standard for volunteers and off-duty firefighters when there was an incident that might require extra personnel. There was no way he'd find a reason to berate her this time, not that that would have stopped her.

She turned on her car's emergency flashers and pressed the accelerator almost to the floor, letting up only when she came to tight corners on the winding, rural road. A full moon added light that upped her confidence, allowing her to drive faster than normal without feeling out of control.

Despite her own speed she noted headlights catching up to her. That driver's flashers were on, too, indicating that he was also part of the rescue in progress. Good. The more hands to do the work, the better, particularly if there were multiple victims.

Sara braked slightly on a corner. The vehicle behind her closed the distance, almost blinding her. Judging by the height and placement of the headlights, she was being followed by a big pickup.

With most of her concentration ahead and a firm grip on the steering wheel, she pushed the gas pedal down harder. The truck not only stayed with her, it was gaining. There was no place to pull over and let him pass. Should she drive faster? Could she keep control if she did?

Another *S*-shaped bend was coming up, this time marked with arrows and a reduced speed limit. She didn't slow that much but she did hold her breath on the curves. The road was built atop a ridge. Sometimes there was a rock wall on one side, sometimes a drop-off, and vice versa. Adrenaline pumping, she sailed through the tight corners with the ability of a racecar driver, praying that no startled whitetail deer would dart in front of her as they sometimes did.

Another corner was coming up. Sara followed the same pattern, slowing just enough to slide around and immediately accelerate. This time, however, she felt a jar. Glanced in the mirror. Saw the truck looming. The fool was too close, coming too fast. "What do you think you're doing?"

In seconds, she knew. He bumped her car again, this time almost causing her to lose control. Heart in her throat, she hit the gas while she tried to recall which of the volunteers drove a similar truck. If this was a stranger, he was either a lousy driver or bent on causing her to wreck. Well, she wasn't going down without a fight!

The blindingly bright image in the mirror drew closer again. Sara battled to keep control of both her car and her emotions. A little more gas? It was that or let herself be tagged again.

Because the truck was clearly much larger and heavier, her only chance of escape was to try to outrun it. On a straight road she'd have had no chance in her little car but on these curves she might win. Seeing his grille glittering in the rearview mirror terrified her. He had to be practically in her trunk!

More gas. Another turn. Her wheels skidded. She knew the moment her tires lost traction. She was done for.

"No!" Sara's car left the road, broke through a barbwire fence and became airborne. For an instant she felt weightless.

Her hands froze on the useless wheel. She held her breath. Saw a stand of cedars ahead with cleared land below her. There was no time for prayer other than to call, "God, help me!"

The car slammed into the ground nose first, bounced ahead to smash into the cedars, and her airbag exploded in her face.

Adam had been killing time at the station, waiting for Sara's shift to end, when the accident call came in. Units from Mountain Grove and Kosh had also been started so he held back, waiting to see if he was needed.

Clay called to him, "You comin', man?"

"If they go to a second alarm." He glanced at his watch. "I have to pick up Sara in a few minutes."

As he watched his coworkers pull out of the station he wished he could be with them, yet knew staying behind was the right decision. There was plenty of coverage already and Sara needed him. Unless…

Adam's gut twisted. Knowing her, she may have chosen to respond in spite of his warnings. There was only one way to find out.

He broke speed limits getting to the hospital, left his truck idling by the emergency entrance and ran inside to the admitting desk.

"Sara Southerland," he said without explanation. "What floor is she on?"

"Second," the young administration clerk replied. "But you won't find her there. She just left."

Adam's heart cracked like an eggshell. "Where did she go?"

"Said something about an accident as she ran past me. Did you check to see if her car is here?"

He hadn't, but it only took a few seconds to remedy that error. Sara was gone, all right. And he knew exactly where she was headed.

The radio in his truck broadcast a cancellation for additional responders before he'd reached the outskirts of town. Adam kept going. If Sara was already on her way she wouldn't know about the recall because her car wasn't equipped with a radio and her pager had been ruined by the first vandalism incident. She'd drive until she reached the scene and learned that additional medics were unneeded. All he had to do was be sure he didn't let her slip past him returning to town in the dark.

Relying on his headlights and the moon, he sped north. The radio toned again. "All units be advised, we have a second report of a TC on Seventeen, off the road at mile marker 134."

A TC, another traffic collision. Adam grabbed the mic. "This is Kane. I'm almost on scene, passing 132."

And then he spotted a flicker of orange. "Be advised, it looks like we may have a fire."

Sara was initially stunned by the crash. She pushed the collapsing airbag away from her face and managed to release her seatbelt. The front doors were both jammed shut by the bend in the car's chassis but she managed to crawl out a broken side window.

She stepped back, tall pasture grass brushing her knees, and began to gape at her poor car as reason returned. "I'm alive! Thank you, Jesus!" Rubbing her sore left shoulder she smiled with relief. "Whoa. That's gonna leave a mark."

Her high spirits fell when she saw bright headlights slowing on the road above her. Was that a Good Samaritan or were the guys who had caused the wreck coming back? There was only one sensible thing to do. Hide. But where? Lying in the long grass was out of the question considering the full moon. That left the trees as the only option.

Trying to avoid the thickest clumps of vegetation so

she wouldn't mash it down and leave a trail, she zigzagged her way to the stand of cedars and ducked beneath pendulous branches. Clouds of pollen enveloped her. She pressed a tissue over her nose and mouth, praying she wouldn't start to sneeze.

Shadows moved. Here they came. Maybe she'd been wrong. One of the two people she could see had lit a flare so they were probably going to mark the spot where she'd left the road and go for help. Or were they?

Sara faded back into the hanging branches. Was that gasoline she smelled? Her gas tank must have ruptured in the crash.

The lit flare bobbed closer in the dark. Then it was flying in an arc, tumbling end over end.

She was giving thanks that it hadn't reached her car when some of the dry undergrowth caught fire. Red and orange embers twinkled like stars, blinking off in seconds. Then others appeared. A circle spread, creeping out from its center. A few well-placed steps would stop it before it did much damage. Only she wasn't in a position to stomp on anything.

And then it was too late. Flames gathered, compounded. The fire raced along the ground to her car, quickly enveloping the rear portion as the man responsible and his partner ran back toward the roadway.

Sara crouched behind a sturdy cedar and thanked the Lord she wasn't trapped in the burning car. Even if it was merely scorched, the fumes might have killed her. If and when the heat reached the ruptured fuel tank her fate would have been decided.

Bystanders' vehicles were gathering along the raised road, making it impossible for her to tell if her assailants had left. Sirens echoed in the hilly terrain, close yet so far. The fire began to hiss as though it were alive. Something was venting! Sara ducked back and covered her face, wishing she'd donned her protective gear before leaving the hospital.

This time, the explosion was more of a muted boom than the loud one when Bessie's oxygen tanks had blown. A flare of burning gasoline reached the nearest cedar branches and set them crackling. In a few more minutes she was going to have to show herself whether her attackers were gone or not.

A distant male voice rose above the rest, shouting, "No!"

She was afraid to peek out for fear of injury. Others were yelling. Somebody screamed, shrill like a woman. A siren approached and wound down. Help had arrived!

Sara worked her way from tree to tree, keeping the cedars between her and the fire. As soon as she judged herself in the clear she scanned the pasture.

A fire engine was up on the road shining spotlights on her car while nozzlemen sprayed the grass from a safe distance to contain the flames. Off to one side, several firefighters in full gear were holding back a man she couldn't help but recognize. Adam struggled valiantly. He kept shouting, "Sara! Sara!" at the top of his lungs.

"Adam, I'm here," she called out, hurrying forward and coughing from the tree pollen and smoke. "I'm here. I'm okay."

His shoulders slumped. The others released him. He came to her in three strides and wrapped his arms around her so tightly she could barely breathe.

As she clung to him she knew this was a temporary respite from the well-deserved scolding she was bound to receive. She didn't care. It was worth being chastised to know how much he cared, to feel his strong arms around her, holding her again. This was different than the time he'd comforted her after her apartment was trashed and different than the way he'd held her when they'd kissed in front of the police department, too.

This was better. Stronger. Deeper. More poignant, yet joyful at the same time. If she had had her way he would never have let go.

Taking a shuddering breath he swept her up in his arms and started for the road. "Are you hurt?"

"I—I don't think so. I had my seatbelt on and the airbag worked."

"You should know better than to drive too fast to a call."

She'd wound both arms around his neck and was holding tight. "It wasn't my fault. There was a truck after me. He kept hitting my bumper. I was trying to outrun him."

"What?" Adam set her on her feet and grasped her shoulders. She winced when he touched the left one so he let go. "I thought you said you weren't hurt."

"Seatbelt, I think," she replied. "It's not serious. I can rotate my arm. See?" She proceeded to demonstrate.

"The truck that hit you. What did it look like?"

"Big. Dark. All I could really see was the high, bright headlights in my mirrors."

She watched his jaw clench and his nostrils flare. *Here it comes.* Doing her best to stand tall and take the deserved criticism she waited. And waited. Finally, Adam scooped her up again, carried her to the rear of the waiting ambulance and handed her over. "Here. See if you can do anything with her. I give up."

Sara was dumbfounded. "Aren't you going to lecture me?"

Instead, he kept going, approached the nearest engine and disappeared behind it.

For once she deserved a good scolding and he didn't

deliver. Truth to tell, he didn't need to. Clearly she had been foolish to let her desire to perform as a medic over-rule her good sense. It had been wrong to leave town, to leave Adam behind. She knew and admitted it. Now all she had to do was apologize and make him believe she'd turned over a new leaf.

That, and find something to drive that I can afford, she added, watching the last of her car go up in flames. "That's what I get for making the last payment."

The medic, Vince, who had disrespected her in the past, spoke more kindly this time. "At least you got out alive."

"Yes. Thank God. Literally," Sara told him, sober-ing. "I don't think the guys after me were supposed to let me escape."

SEVENTEEN

Adam lingered at the accident scene to make sure Sara was well taken care of. He didn't trust himself to speak while he was coping with his rollercoaster emotions. Trying to watch out for Sara was akin to rounding up a bunch of wild yearling calves that didn't have the sense to come in out of a hailstorm.

Oh, she was intelligent. He didn't doubt that. But he couldn't figure out exactly what drove her to take risks the way she had when she was younger. Recently she seemed to be behaving even more erratically. Could it be because of losing Vicki?

That notion mellowed him appreciably. Every loss in life made a difference, just as triumphs did. It was how people dealt with uncontrollable events that developed their character. For him, his Christian faith had provided the answers to most of his questions and he firmly believed that the things he didn't understand were nevertheless going to work out for his good. The Bible promised they would. The hard part was waiting for it to happen.

Medics had been administering oxygen to Sara at the rear of the ambulance. When they removed the mask and Adam was able to clearly see her face, he felt a jolt that hit him like a sucker punch. Not rejoining her was unthinkable. What he would say to her was his only conundrum.

Unsure what to expect, he tried to stroll leisurely toward her and found it impossible to slow his pace. All he wanted was to be with her, to touch her hand, to make sure she was truly all right despite the accident. By the time she noticed him and smiled, his anxiety had pushed him into a jog.

Sara raised both palms as if surrendering. "Don't say it. I already know I was nuts to drive out here alone."

"I don't intend to say a thing," Adam replied. "What happened to your car made the point for me." He swallowed past the lump in his throat and reached to grasp her hand. "I'm thankful that's all you lost tonight."

"Me, too. When I was flying through the air I wasn't sure how I was going to land. The airbag and those cedars saved me."

He shook his head, capturing her gaze and holding it. "You could have wrecked anywhere out here and ended up dead. Losing control on that specific corner is more likely divine intervention than happenstance."

To Sara's credit she looked penitent. "You're right. I'm pretty sure I thanked God when I realized I'd survived. To tell you the truth, I don't remember much except driving as fast as I could and praying for deliverance."

"Why did you decide to hide in the trees?"

"Instinct for self-preservation." Shrugging, she winced, her pain evident. "I had no idea those two guys were going to torch my car but I knew they were bad news."

Adam tensed. "Wait. The fire was deliberate, too?"

"Yes." She was nodding slowly. "When the smoke dies down and it's daylight, tell Chief Ellis to look directly between the road and my car, about twenty feet from where it burned. He should find the remnants of a burned-out flare unless the pressure from the nozzles washed it away."

When Sara was being so professional about the clues he didn't want to stop her, yet the urge to pull her into an embrace and just hold her was strong. "What else?"

"Nothing else. The truck came out of nowhere and followed me. It was big. Probably a three-quarter ton. They kept ramming my car until I lost control and crashed. After that they came back, lit a road flare and tossed it into the dry grass."

Urging her closer, Adam asked, "Did you recognize them?"

"No," Sara answered with a tremor in her tone. Adam opened his arms to her. She stepped into his waiting embrace. Her cheek was against his chest when she said, "I truly am sorry I didn't listen to you."

"Shush, honey. You aren't badly hurt. That's the important thing." He was stroking her back, brushing off bits of cedar twigs as he did so. "I'll run you by ER so you can have a doc check your shoulder."

"I don't need..." Breaking off, she raised her face to him and smiled before saying, "Yes, Adam. I think that's a great idea."

He huffed a chuckle. "Who *are* you, lady, and what have you done with Sara?"

The worst part about visiting the ER was the teasing she took from her coworkers once they realized her injury was superficial. It was really embarrassing to listen to Adam adding funny comments to the already humorous conversation going on around her.

"Yup," he said, grinning. "The car's a real fixer-upper. A little paint, a few dents hammered out and it'll be—"

"Good as new?" the ER doctor guessed.

Adam laughed so Sara shot him a pseudo-angry glare. "Try a total wreck no matter what. There's nothing wrong with my poor car that being melted down and recycled won't cure."

"Ah, sorry." The doctor backed off and jotted notes on an iPad. "I don't think anything is broken. I'll give you an off-work order for now and a prescription for painkillers. See me or your regular physician when you think you're ready to go back to work."

"I'm ready now."

"You won't be by tomorrow when the full extent of your bruising hits you. Trust me. It's gonna get a lot worse."

Sara chortled. "Did anybody ever tell you you have a lousy bedside manner, doc?"

"Only every nurse I've ever met," he joked back. "But you all are notoriously hard to please."

"I'd take more offense if we were all female," Sara teased. She singled out Adam. "As soon as everybody is done making fun of me would you please drive me out to the ranch? I seem to be on foot."

"That you are. Would you like to borrow one of my horses for transportation?"

"And ride it to work? Sure. That would be peachy."

"At least the horse would be smart enough to stay on the trail."

She made a face at him and slid off the exam table. "That would be funnier if I hadn't just paid off that car. I'm not looking forward to trying to replace it with what the insurance will give me."

He cupped her elbow. "Understood. Let's worry about one thing at a time. I'll take you home for now. Tomorrow we can go back to the accident scene if you want and look for clues—after the sheriff's people are done."

"My purse was in the car. I don't have a driver's license or a credit card or a cent to my name until the bank opens."

"I'll take care of you," Adam said.

Sara's initial reaction was to bristle and argue. She squelched the urge, determined to behave amiably. It wasn't Adam's fault she needed help right now and his offer was a kind thing to do. Her problem was being in a position where she was forced to accept assistance instead of insisting she was in control. "Thanks."

To her surprise, he laughed.

Brows knitting, she scowled at him. "What?"

"Nothing. I'm amazed you didn't choke on your thank-you, that's all."

"I thought I was hiding my feelings. Guess I'm not as good at it as I figured."

"Sometimes you are," Adam said as he ushered her out to his truck. "Like when you had me convinced you weren't interested in romance."

"Oh?" Struggling to keep her voice even she kept pace. "What changed your mind?"

"Humph. That's a tough question. I'm not sure when I tumbled. It may have been the first time I kissed you."

"That was pretty convincing." Sara was glad the parking lot wasn't too brightly lit because she knew she was blushing.

"Yeah, it sure was." He helped her into his truck and shut the door. Sara watched him circle to the driver's side, appreciating the way he moved, the way he looked—everything about him. And it wasn't only Adam's outward appearance that impressed her. The glimpses she'd gotten into his heart had drawn her to him even more. He was a good man. An honest man. Someone to admire as well as love.

Yes, she admitted without reservation. She loved him.

And she was pretty sure he felt the same about her. Time would tell. As long as he was so committed to protecting her it was hard for her to separate his varying emotions. Maybe he was having the same trouble. Granted they were old friends, but this aspect of their relationship was new. It needed exploring without being affected by outward trauma.

As he slid behind the wheel she smiled at him.

He scowled. "What?"

"I'm just happy to be alive—and to be with you."

"Even though I'm bossy?"

"Uh-huh."

Adam made a silly face at her. "I'm never going to figure you out, am I?"

Sara laughed. "Probably not. I haven't figured myself out yet so why should you be able to?"

If his truck had had an old-fashioned bench seat instead of bucket seats with a console between, Adam would have pulled Sara closer and tucked her under his arm. Even a narrow space of separation was too far to suit him.

His thoughts were churning more than the thunderheads highlighted by the moonlight. "What's your best guess about the truck that rammed you?"

"I don't have a clue, Adam. I wish I did."

"How about the two guys who got out and started the fire?"

"What about them?"

"Were they tall, short, big, little—what?"

He heard her sigh and glanced over. Sara had her eyes shut, her head resting on the back of the seat, hopefully visualizing the scene.

"One was taller than the other," she finally said. "And he seemed more athletic. I mean, he moved faster."

"Okay. That's something. What else?"

"The short one lagged behind. I think I saw him trip a couple of times. I'm not sure. By that time I was mostly watching the lit flare."

"Maybe they didn't mean to drop it." He was hoping to soothe her but his comment had the opposite effect.

"Oh, they meant to, all right." Sara shuddered and hugged herself. "Now that I think about it, they seemed to be fighting, too. The short guy caught up to the taller one and grabbed for the flare. They struggled for a second, then almost dropped it right there."

"And?"

Turning to stare at him, Sara gasped. "It was like one of them wanted to set my car on fire and the other one didn't. The little guy got hold of the flare, wound up like a pitcher and threw it, end over end. It wasn't much of a throw, though. I hoped it would land short, and it did. But the grass was dry and there was enough fire to set off the spilled fuel."

"What about voices? Could you hear their argument?"

"I don't remember. I'm sorry. Part of the time I was hiding I had to hug a tree just to stay on my feet."

"What about afterward? Did they stay to watch?"

She brightened. "I don't think so. They ran for the road. The big guy was practically dragging the little one."

"By the hand?"

Sara's jaw dropped. "Yes. At least that's the impression I got."

"That's interesting."

"It sure is. If Rigo and Hector brought a girl with them we've been looking for the wrong people."

Adam was coming to a slightly different conclusion,

which he kept to himself. He would, however, share his ideas with Chief Magill or Sheriff Caruthers, once he decided which of them was most likely to investigate subtly.

First, though, the police were going to have to make Hector confess and fill them in on his cohorts. Until that happened, Adam intended to keep his crazy notions to himself. In a small town like Paradise, where everybody and his brother were related in some way, he had to worry about local politics. If he intended to keep living and working there, which he did, Adam knew he'd best tread lightly.

One more thing was clear. Getting Sara on board with his various ideas was going to be next to impossible without proof. Right now she seemed amenable to his sensible suggestions. If he gave her another strong reason to fight him, however, he was pretty sure she'd stop being so easy to get along with.

He couldn't have that. Not when her life might very well depend upon how well she paid attention to him.

EIGHTEEN

Sara was so exhausted she dozed off on the ride to the Kane ranch. Changes in the truck's motion roused her enough to unbuckle her seatbelt when they arrived. Adam got out and opened the passenger door. She was turning, preparing to step down, when he slipped his arms around her and lifted.

Weariness brought an unconvincing, "I can walk."

"Yup. But I'm going to carry you."

"Mmm." She slipped an arm around his neck and rested her cheek on his chest. This was so like her dream of a handsome cowboy rescuing her she almost slipped back into that lovely fantasy. "Where's your white Stetson?"

"I left it with my horse," he quipped. "I'm in firefighter mode right now."

"Works for me."

Shouldering his way in the front door, Adam gently placed her on the sofa then went to the base of the staircase to call out, "Hey, Kurt, we're home."

"He's probably asleep like normal folks are at this time of the morning," Sara said with a lopsided smile. "I'll try not to wake him but I have to take a shower. Cedar pollen in my hair is driving me crazy." As proof, she sniffled and sneezed.

"I believe you," Adam said. "If you see Kurt, tell him I went to check the barn." He paused. "Can you get up the stairs all right?"

"I told you the only thing that hurts is my shoulder," she insisted, making her voice sweet so he wouldn't think she was complaining. "I can't tell you how thankful I am to be here, to be *anywhere*, after the wreck tonight."

He hooked his thumbs in the pockets of his jeans and nodded. "Me, too. It's been a long time since I've been that scared. When I saw your car on fire I thought…"

"That's the only reason I showed myself as quickly as I did," she replied. "I could tell how worried you were."

"Yeah, well." He was backing away. "Take care. I'll lock the front door and catch the back when I'm done in the barn."

Pushing herself to her feet she paused to study him. "Are you concerned about your animals? I mean, do you think whoever is stalking me will bother them?"

"No." He glanced toward a living room window. "It looks like there's a storm brewing and I need to make sure everything is secured. Lightning and thunder can get horses really riled up. Besides, either Kurt or I make rounds every night before we turn in."

"Maybe he already did it."

"I just need to unwind, okay?"

"Okay, then. Good night." She stretched and headed for the stairs, knowing that if she looked back and saw Adam lingering below she'd be sorely tempted to volunteer for another hug. Or two. Being around him had always been nice. Now it was so much more. When he was nearby the air was fresher, the sun shone brighter, the world seemed safer even if nothing else had changed.

Putting one foot after the other she made it to the second floor. Bright moonlight shone through her bedroom windows, drawing her to enter and look below. Except for a few blowing leaves and eddies of dust, everything seemed peaceful in the front yard, but she needed to find a different window in order to see the barn. It was time to watch over Adam as he often watched over her.

Passing the open door to the room he was currently sharing with his brother, Sara noticed that although one of the beds looked slept in, there was nobody there now. She paused. "Kurt?"

One of the upstairs bathrooms was directly across the hall. That door stood open as well. "Kurt? Where are you?"

No one answered. Sara started to get antsy. Kurt should have been in the house. If he, too, was in the barn Adam would meet up with him and everything would be fine. If not? If not, Adam needed to be warned.

Remembering the way he'd lectured her for phoning him when he'd been searching for trespassers she hesitated momentarily. *Don't be ridiculous. Finding Kurt and keeping Adam safe is far more important*, she told herself.

She patted the pocket of her scrub smock and was relieved to find her cell had not fallen out during the crash. If it had been in her purse, it, too, would have melted in the car fire.

The phone was showing only 21 percent charge so she hurriedly tapped the screen to contact Adam. His phone rang. And rang. Could he have left it in his truck? She ended that call and repeated it. Nothing but ringing. "Come on, Adam. Answer me."

Fine hairs on the back of Sara's neck prickled. The old house creaked as if sympathizing with its absent owners. Wind penetrated invisible cracks, whistling, softly moaning. She didn't believe in ghosts but she was in tune with her intuition and *that* was telling her something was very wrong.

"It might be nothing," she murmured, trying to convince herself she was getting uptight for no reason.

"Yeah, and it might be another sneak attack," she said more firmly. She didn't know where Adam and Kurt kept their firearms but she had seen sports equipment in the closet of the room she was occupying. Surely something in there would do for defense.

Armed with an aluminum baseball bat that was so dirty and scarred up it had probably belonged to the Kane boys when they were kids, Sara held it as if she were anticipating a pitch and started back down the stairway.

Should she call out to either brother again? Kurt obviously wasn't upstairs and, given her lack of information about the current situation, she decided against making her presence known any more than she already had.

Her fingers were gripping the bat so tightly they hurt. Perspiration dotted her forehead and trickled down her temples. Sweaty palms didn't help her grip. The unfamiliar shadows in the house didn't subdue her vivid imagination, either. It was all she could do to settle herself enough to make it through the kitchen to the back door.

Once she ventured outside she'd be in the open, she realized. There were lights dimly shining out the wide doorway of the barn, though, so Adam must be close by. All she had to do was get to him and they could search for Kurt together.

A tear joined the drops slipping from her forehead. She blotted them against her shoulder. *My fault. My fault*, her mind kept insisting. The one person she cared most about in the whole world was in jeopardy because she'd accepted his assistance instead of standing on her own two feet.

Joining that thought was the remembrance of her dear cousin Vicki. She had been dauntless. Courageous enough to face both a flood and thieves. And she was quite dead.

* * *

When Adam first entered the barn he braced the loose door back to stop it from swinging closed and banging in the wind. Nothing seemed amiss.

As he progressed, keen senses heightened his awareness. Horses who usually greeted his arrival with soft snorts and nickers seemed unduly uneasy. Some pawed the floors of their stalls. Others tossed their heads, ears back, as if preparing to face a pack of ravenous wolves. Were they reacting to the approaching storm? Or did their fear have a different cause? And where were the usually omnipresent farm dogs?

Adam hefted a pitchfork. It would be useless against a gun but was enough to make him feel armed. To send his memories of foreign battlegrounds whirling like an Ozark tornado. His body reacted instinctively. He dropped into a crouch and proceeded with caution, keeping his back to the wall where bales of alfalfa hay were stacked.

A door slammed outside. Car? House? Was Sara up to her usual escapades? He dearly hoped not, because the hair on the nape of his neck was prickling the way it had when he and his unit had been ordered to enter a supposedly deserted village where every structure might hide an enemy. Every unidentified shadow be lethal.

He froze, listening. What was that? A moan? Were his ears playing tricks on him?

The head and shoulders of a small person appeared at the outer edge of the wide open doorway. Her long, silky hair was lifted and fanned by the wind. *Sara!* Adam wanted to shout at her, to run and grab her to keep her from entering. Circumstances recommended neither. At this point, the best move was to show himself and draw attention his way, just in case the horses were right.

Adam straightened. "Stop!" He saw her falter, retreat a bit, then come forward again. "Stop, I said."

"Adam?"

"Stay out there." His jaw clenched, as did his fists enclosing the handle of the makeshift weapon.

"Is Kurt with you?"

What kind of a question was that? He shivered. "Why?"

"Because I can't find him."

"Get back in the house!" Adam hoped he didn't sound as frantic as he felt.

"By myself?"

She had a good point, one he couldn't ignore. "All right. Stay right there. I'm coming to you."

She disappeared back around the corner. He reached the door in five long strides and whipped around the edge.

Sara was waiting with an old baseball bat poised over her shoulder. She halted her swing just as he ducked. "Adam!"

Relieving her of the bat he drew her close with one arm, keeping their backs to the wall. "Are you sure Kurt isn't in the house?"

"I looked all over upstairs. And I hollered for him. He didn't answer."

"That doesn't explain why you're out here." Tense before, every muscle was now as taut as a lasso around the neck of a fighting, frenzied bull.

Sara was clinging to his side. "I had to tell you. Why didn't you answer your phone? I tried to call before I came outside."

"I'd turned the ringer off. Didn't feel it vibrate."

"Have you seen your brother out here?"

"No. But I did think I heard a funny noise before you

showed up." He pivoted. "Get behind me and stay there. I can't leave you out here, exposed."

"Do you think it was Kurt you heard?"

"Maybe. Maybe not. Something sure has the horses wound up tonight. And I don't see any of the dogs."

He started forward, feeling Sara's presence and trying to keep from paying too much attention to her. His focus must be on whoever or whatever was lurking in the barn or they'd be in worse danger than before.

Truth to tell, Adam would rather have escorted Sara back to the house but if his brother wasn't at home he felt he had no choice but to proceed.

The strength of the wind had increased and begun to lift and spin loose straw from the dirt floor and the tops of the stored hay bales. It didn't decrease visibility much but it was a distraction.

Soothing each horse in turn, Adam led Sara along the bank of stalls. Several on the end were empty. Those, he approached with added caution.

Suddenly there was a sharp cry from the last stall. The air was filled with movement, bodies, screeching, flying bits of straw and talons.

Adam staggered back, startled.

Sara screamed, threw her arms in front of her face and ducked low.

Adam lost his footing and tumbled over her arched back. She screamed again. And again.

Hardly able to think, let alone reason, Sara was finally able to regain functional self-control. It was recognizing the reddish colors of their attackers and the flying bunches of ruffled feathers that brought comprehension.

She began to laugh hysterically. They had just been assaulted by a flock of roosting chickens!

A quick glance at Adam quieted her. "What? That was funny, okay?"

"Not if your stalkers are what spooked them," he grumbled, getting to his feet and cautiously approaching the closed half door to the stall. "Back off."

She complied. Her body was trembling and her agitated thoughts reminded her of a load of clothes in a washing machine. Adam. Kurt. Stalkers. Night. Darkness. A wreck. A burning car. Back to Adam. And Kurt.

The crazy actions of that bunch of misguided chickens had nothing on her brain. Her gaze tracked Adam's every step. Watched his hand release the catch on the stall's lower door. Saw him slowly pull it open.

Adam shouted and disappeared through the opening. Sara almost turned and ran. Instead, she hefted the pitchfork he'd dropped and tiptoed closer. Could she actually stab someone with it if she had to?

Praying silently she crept closer and saw Adam. He was hunched over something on the floor in the loose straw. It was his missing brother!

"Is—is he okay?" she managed to stutter.

"Yes. He's tied up but otherwise fine."

The sound of ripping tape proved that conclusion as Kurt's mouth was freed.

"Did you see who grabbed you?" Adam asked.

Kurt continued to shout until Sara interrupted. "Hi."

"Sorry," the younger man said. He got to his feet with Adam's help. "No, I didn't see who it was. There were at least two, maybe three."

"How long ago?" Sara asked.

"Felt like hours. What time is it now?"

"Almost dawn." She huffed. "It could have happened before my wreck."

Kurt was rubbing his wrists. "What wreck?"

"It's a long story," she said, bracing with her back to the inside of the stall. "Did you hear the people who grabbed you leave or are they still around?"

"Long gone." Kurt brushed himself off. "Can we talk about this in the kitchen? I missed my supper."

Words of agreement were not necessary. All Sara had to do was make eye contact with Adam and she had the okay.

"What about the dogs?" Kurt asked as they left the barn together. "Did you see them?"

Sara winced. "No. You don't think they were hurt, do you?"

"I'm not sure," Kurt said. "When I first came outside to see why they were barking, they were all staggering around like they were drunk. Or drugged."

"Oh, no!" Unshed tears filled her eyes. Nobody had the right to take out their anger on helpless animals.

Adam had finished securing the barn, caught up and reached for her hand. She let him hold it. "It's almost sunup. We'll go look for them when we can see better."

"We need to find them now. They may need a vet." Tears had begun to stream down her cheeks. "This is too much. It's all too much. It's not fair."

"You've got that right," Adam replied, leaning into the increasing wind. "It isn't fair. Come on. Let's all go inside where it's quieter. We need to call the sheriff and report what happened to Kurt."

Although Sara nodded, wiped her tears and let him tug her along she wasn't eager to give up on the missing dogs. Then she noticed something. "Where'd Kurt go? He was right next to us."

The young man's voice sounded muffled when he called, "Over here. I found old Charlie and the others under the porch. They're groggy but breathing fine."

Sara gasped with joy. She wasn't sure whether it was considered okay to pray for animals or not, but she had been doing just that. And Kurt had brought her answer almost before she'd said, *Amen*. The humans embroiled in this mess may still be in jeopardy, but at least the innocent animals had come through it all right. At least she hoped so.

It wasn't a huge triumph but it was something good. At this point, she was willing to praise the Lord for the tiniest blessing.

And there lay the deeper lesson, she mused. While waiting for answers to her grand prayers, she was missing small daily joys that lifted a believer's spirits and brought peace despite trials. Like the touch of Adam Kane's strong hand.

NINETEEN

Kurt ended up making breakfast for his brother, Sara, Sheriff Caruthers and Deputy Elmer Ott, aka Tiger, after they finished checking the crime scene. Rain was falling.

"More pancakes, anybody?" he asked, gesturing with a spatula.

Adam was too engrossed in the sheriff's report to eat much. He waved the request away and continued asking questions. "You're positive Hector gave you good intel?"

"Oh, yeah. All he wants is to be sent back to Texas and leave us crazy hillbillies behind." Caruthers' grin was wide and genuine, helping to relieve some of Adam's angst.

"Okay, what about his three buddies? Was one really a woman?"

"A teenage girl. We picked them all up. Once we had a vehicle description it wasn't hard to locate their SUV. The girl folded and explained everything the minute we started interrogating her. They came up here to make sure Vicki hadn't passed on any evidence or told anyone about their illegal enterprises."

Sara interrupted. "Which one shot Rigo and why? And who set Vicki's place on fire?"

Caruthers shrugged. "Hard to tell. They're all blaming each other for his death to keep law enforcement confused. The only thing they do agree on is shooting to miss you."

"*Miss* me?" Sara's eyes widened.

"Yup. The idea was to scare you so you'd tell the truth when they questioned you. They swear they never used a rifle."

Adam leaned forward, elbows on the kitchen table. "Whoa. How can that be? I mean, the slugs you dug out of the tree were fired from a rifle, right?"

"Looked like it to me. Haven't gotten ballistics info back from Jeff City yet, though." He slurped his coffee, then held out the cup for more as Kurt brought a carafe to the table. "Thing is, they did confess to shooting your truck in town and following you back here to the ranch. That's how they knew where Sara was staying."

She interrupted. "So, why trash my apartment? I mean, if they were looking for Vicki's journal, why make such a mess of the place when they didn't find it?"

Caruthers shook his head thoughtfully. "Beats me. They admit to tossing the place but deny spilling any paint. Hector said they thought Vicki might have given proof of the thefts to you and they were hoping to scare you enough to give it back."

"When? How?"

"Out here, tonight, apparently. Only you weren't home."

Adam watched Sara's face, wondering if she had come to the same conclusions he had. Finally, he said, "This doesn't make sense. They had already tied up Kurt and drugged the dogs. Why didn't they wait?"

"I think because Hector had been their leader. Without him in charge, they got into an argument and bailed too soon." The sheriff smiled behind his coffee mug. "You should be glad."

"We are." Adam covered Sara's hand with his. "I just

wish I could connect all the dots. Didn't they have a second car? There were two of them when we came under fire at Sara's first apartment."

"It broke down and they abandoned it," Deputy Ott offered. "I was having it towed to impound when we got the call to come out here. Haven't had a chance to go over it yet."

Sighing heavily, Adam nodded. "Okay. What now?"

"More questioning," Caruthers said, draining his cup and setting it aside. "We'll sort out who murdered their cohort and put together a time line before long. In the meantime, staying here and keeping your heads down is probably the most sensible move."

Kurt saluted with his coffee mug. "I'll drink to that."

Unsatisfied, Adam got to his feet and followed the sheriff and his deputy to the kitchen door. Rain was still dripping off the eaves and had left muddy puddles, while more menacing, dark clouds raced across the morning sky. "Are you positive you got them all? I mean, couldn't there be other gang members out there with an ax to grind toward Sara?"

"Could be, but I doubt it," the sheriff replied. "These guys are good for all her troubles. It's just a matter of figuring out which ones were on scene when they happened."

"Meaning, you think they split up and could be responsible for everything? Even running her off the road?"

"Exactly. One person couldn't be in all those places at once but an organized gang could have covered it." He patted Adam's shoulder in passing. "Quit worrying, son. I've got this."

"If you say so." Still, Adam wasn't satisfied. He was the kind of direct thinker who liked all his facts to mesh neatly. These didn't.

He trailed the lawmen outside and stood on the porch. "Don't forget to ask them who slashed Sara's tires and left the note on the windshield."

Caruthers waved and slammed the door of his car while Elmer got into the patrol unit and also drove away.

Sensing Sara close behind him, Adam turned and slipped a protective arm around her. "You cold?"

Sara nodded. "Yes. But the rain's letting up. Before we go in I want to check on your poor dogs again. They might be cold and wet."

"It's the nurse in you, I suppose. Fair enough. Come on." He led her down the steps to the side of the porch that opened into a makeshift den for the recovering dogs.

Despite the cloudy morning, a porch light sent parallel bars of illumination through slits between the boards. She crouched to peer underneath. "They're wagging their tails, especially that little one that looks like a beagle. Maybe the bigger dogs kept him from eating as much of whatever Hector's gang fed them to knock them out."

"Maybe."

"I don't suppose you'd let me take them all inside and pamper them until they're on their feet?" She brushed her hair off her face and peered up at him.

"They're not housebroken, so, no. They'll be fine where they are. Being in the house when they're not used to it would make them too nervous. Let them rest here, where they're comfortable."

Leaning back she raised a hand and Adam helped her stand. "*Now* are you ready to go in?"

"Um—" her glance traveled to the barn "—I know Deputy Elmer didn't find much evidence but maybe we should look for ourselves."

"They bagged the duct tape that was wrapped around Kurt. What else could there be?" Adam knew the moment he asked the question that Sara was going to come up with a contradiction. He could see it in her expression, in her sparkling eyes.

She began to grin. "If I knew what to look for I'd have told Elmer. That's why clues are part of a mystery."

"You're the mystery," Adam said. He couldn't help returning her smile. Resiliency was one of Sara's best traits. Well, that and her wit, her intellect and her caring heart. Nursing was the perfect career for her.

"Let's go take a look," she urged. "You can check your horses again while I poke around everywhere else."

"Play with the kittens, you mean?"

One shoulder rose in a casual shrug and she chuckled. "Well, that, too."

As long as Sara kept her mind on animals and on her search for obscure clues she stayed pretty calm, at least outwardly. The times she slipped and recalled finding Kurt bound and gagged, she trembled all the way from the top of her head to the muddy soles of her shoes.

It was harder to be at her best when she was even a short distance away from Adam. Consequently, she dogged his footsteps from stall to stall until he came to the one where they'd found his brother. That was where she stopped, turning her back while he explored alone.

Interior lights were on but didn't fully illuminate the darkest corners. Sara was glad to see a few beams from the rising sun peek through the clouds. Violent spring storms were normal in the Ozarks. Whether this one was done or would redevelop and slam into them again was fifty-fifty. Weather could go from sunny to threatening in less than half an hour, and often did.

A soft stirring amid the stacked hay bales drew her away from Adam. She was cooing like a mother to her baby as she approached. "Are you there, kitties? Yes, you are. What good babies. So pretty, so soft."

Rather than reach into the narrow space right away she paused so the kittens could size her up. "It's me, guys. See? Remember?"

Three sets of sky blue eyes blinked up at her. Striped gray and black, the kittens' camouflage was perfect for their shady den. If she had not known where to look she might have missed them. Fortunately, their mother wasn't home at the time or Sara would have had to face hissing and claws.

She slowly took a seat on one of the bales and dangled her fingertips beside it. Something tickled. A soft paw batted at her. *Almost*, she thought. *I've almost won your confidence.*

Two of the bright-eyed babies stayed interested in her. The third acted preoccupied with a black object that looked like a ribbon. Moving in slow motion to keep from frightening her new animal friends, Sara slipped her hand into the narrow space between the bales.

That kitten growled, making her smile. "Good for you, little guy. Stick up for yourself," she whispered. After a short pause she probed farther until she touched his odd plaything. Happily, it was inert rather than being a dead critter his mama had brought her babies for food.

She pinched it between two fingers and drew it out. The hissing kitten made one last effort to grab his toy before it was out of reach.

"Adam?" Sara's voice wasn't loud but it apparently carried enough weight because he joined her immediately.

"What?"

"I'm not sure." Fingering the fabric object she examined it. "What is this thing?"

"I don't know. A ribbon?"

"Not exactly. It looks like one of those bracelets teenagers weave and exchange as tokens of friendship. Do you suppose one of the Texas gang dropped it here?"

"If they did, you shouldn't be handling it," he warned.

"The kitties have been playing with it. I hardly think there'd be DNA or anything else left on it."

"Maybe it's been in here a long time. Or maybe it was stuck to the hay when this load was delivered. It could have come from anywhere."

Sobering, Sara nodded. "You're right."

"Are you ready to go back into the house?"

"I suppose so."

She wadded up the thin bracelet and stuffed it into her pocket. "I still think we may be missing something."

"I'll tell you what I think you're missing—sleep. We've all been so keyed up it's a wonder anybody can string together a whole sentence. It's time you got some rest."

Sara nodded, hurrying to match his longer strides toward the ranch house. "Only if it finally comes with a shower. I still smell smoky from the car fire and I don't like it."

There wasn't enough volume to Adam's chuckle to carry it above the lingering weather noise and huffing of stabled horses but she saw he was amused. "What's so funny?"

"You are," he said. "I'm so used to smoke I hadn't even noticed. It's a firefighter thing."

"Well, it isn't *my* thing," she countered, trying to sound miffed and failing.

"I get it," he teased. "You like medicinal odors. Personally, I prefer smoke or even Kurt's favorite, horses. Just smelling a hospital gives me the willies." He grew somber. "I guess it reminds me of the buddies I visited after they were wounded. And that reminds me of the ones who never came home."

Sara wiped her feet on the mat and preceded him through the kitchen door, then stopped and turned, slipping both arms around his waist. "That was then. This is now. You need to try to put all that aside and concentrate on the future."

Adam's reaction was far from what she had anticipated. Instead of opening his arms and drawing her into his embrace he grasped her shoulders and set her away. "The same goes for you, Sara. We both need to get past what happened to Vicki and everything else that's piled up since, otherwise we'll never be sure of anything." He paused and studied her expression. "I refuse to take advantage of you when you're emotionally overwrought." That said, he walked off.

Sara was stunned. Her dear friend Adam had become much more to her than a simple childhood crush. He had hugged her patiently as she wept. Had even kissed her. So why was she continuing to get mixed signals from him? After all, he had acted jealous of his own brother. He'd also recently pulled her out of more than one trap. Was he getting sick of rescuing her? Was that it?

No matter how many ideas she processed regarding Adam's changeable temperament, she was sure of one thing. He had to be ruing the day he'd become so closely involved in her troubles. It had already cost him his truck window and brought injuries to his younger brother, not to mention the danger they shared every time he was around her. So who had been taking advantage of whom?

And yet, circumstances had her trapped. There was nowhere else to go and nobody she could turn to the way she did Adam Kane. He was one of a kind. A special friend. A person who had proved himself over and over, at home and as a marine. No wonder she'd developed loving feelings toward him. He was easy to like, easy to trust—and easy to love.

Lost in thought, she began to finger the black woven bracelet in her pocket. *I've see this somewhere before*, she told herself, pulling it out and studying it. *But where? When?*

She supposed it was possible that her imagination was providing erroneous information simply because she wanted to put an end to her trials. To dot all the *i*'s and cross all the *t*'s. If she could get a look at the young woman the sheriff had in custody maybe that would bring it all together and make sense. Rigo, she'd known. Hector was also familiar. As for the other two men and the teenage girl, who knew?

Picturing the bracelet on a wrist, she laid it over hers and stared. Unless it had belonged to a very skinny man it had to be a woman's because it was so short.

Sara closed her eyes. The vision wavered like a mirage on a hot day, never becoming clear.

"I *have* seen it," she insisted to herself. "I know I have. All I need to do is remember."

A shiver zinged up her spine and raised gooseflesh on her arms. It wasn't enough to recall seeing the fabric bracelet. She had to know where, when and, most of all, on whose wrist.

And the sooner she unearthed that memory, the sooner she and everyone dear to her could get back to normal.

Even if being normal meant Adam and I wouldn't be forced close together anymore? Sara asked her heart.

The unwelcome answer was *yes*.

TWENTY

After a phone conversation with Sheriff Caruthers the following day, Adam knew what he had to do. Repeated official pleas for the journal Vicki had kept had done no good. Until law enforcement could get a warrant for it and force Helen to turn it over, the case against the gang from Texas was in limbo. Without proof it was going to be tough to charge most of them with more than malicious mischief.

Whoever had shot Rigo and started the fire was the only person facing serious charges. Unfortunately, there was no solid evidence pointing to a specific killer and Caruthers argued that all four were unlikely to have been involved because at least one of them had shot at Sara. Adam didn't agree with that theory because of its timing but he wasn't in charge; the sheriff was.

Pacing the yard outside the barn where Sara was playing with the kittens, Adam took matters into his own hands. He phoned Will Babcock at work.

"Paradise Savings and Loan. How may I direct your call?"

"Will Babcock," Adam said. "It's important."

In seconds, Will was on the line. "Hello?"

"Will, it's Adam Kane. I need to talk to you."

The pause was longer than Adam liked but he finally did get a reply. "You need a loan?"

"What *I* need is unimportant. It's what the police need that matters." Adam cleared his throat. "Is there any way you can convince your mother to turn over your sister's journal?"

"Why? It's just personal ramblings."

"Is it? Have you looked for yourself?"

"I didn't have to," Will said flatly. "My mother told me what's in it."

"Did she also tell you that the chief of police and sheriff have both asked repeatedly to borrow it?"

"What? No. When?"

"The last time was right after he arrested four people from Texas that he believes could be responsible for Vicki's death."

"My sister drowned."

"I don't think so," Adam said, enunciating each word clearly and stretching the spaces between for greater effect.

"Humph. I know what you're trying to do, Kane." Will was adamant. "You're trying to convince everybody that your girlfriend is innocent. Well, I know better. Sara should have stuck with Vicki and she didn't. There's nothing more to say."

"Wait! Don't hang up. Hear me out. If you don't, you'll never know for sure." Listening, Adam didn't hear the desk phone slam down so he continued. "Vicki uncovered graft in the records she was asked to keep in Texas. The original receipts were lost in the flood but we believe she wrote everything down in her journal."

"What makes you think that?"

"Habits," Adam replied. "She was always making notes. If she hadn't been so methodical she might not have noticed the thefts. According to Sara, large quantities of goods meant for flood victims had disappeared. Vicki was positive she'd figured out who was responsible but she died before she could prove it."

"So what good is her journal?"

"It can point to motive and give the police more reason to hold the prisoners until they sort this all out."

"You're going out on a limb," Will told Adam. "Even if Vicki did have suspicions, suppose there are no details written down? That would make it look like Sara is inventing excuses for herself."

"I'll take that chance," Adam said. "How about it? Can you get the journal to the sheriff or police chief?"

Again there was an uncomfortable silence. "Maybe," Will said with a sigh. "I won't promise a thing until I've talked to my mother. It's up to her. She's already suffered enough and I'm not going to upset her if I can help it."

"Understood." He cleared his throat. "The sheriff is trying to get a warrant for it but the sooner, the better. Don't you think it would be easier on Helen if she turned it over on her own? It is inevitable."

"I see. All right. I'll sit down with her this evening and see what I can do."

"Thanks, man." Adam's hopes rose. He didn't want any of the people who had accosted Sara to be released, there or back in Texas. The only way to be certain she remained safe was to break up the theft operation for good.

Plus, it is the right thing to do, Adam added to himself. Those supplies and the money behind them had been donated for disaster relief. Anybody who knowingly took advantage of that system deserved to land in jail. And stay there.

Sara was playing with the kittens when Adam entered the barn. His smile didn't reach his eyes. That was disappointing. "I wondered when you were going to come looking for me," she said.

"I knew exactly where you were."

That brought a soft chuckle. "I don't doubt that for a second. Did I hear you talking outside?"

He nodded. "Yeah. I called Will Babcock."

"What for?"

"I thought maybe he could talk Helen into turning over Vicki's journal instead of waiting for a warrant."

"Um, did it work?"

"Time will tell."

Thoughtful, Sara nodded and focused back on the kittens in her lap. "I was wondering… When I can finally go home, would you let me take one of these babies with me as a pet? I'd really like having the company."

He had busied himself arranging unused halters on pegs nearby and barely glanced over his shoulder. "Sure. No problem."

Joy filled her thank-you and brought unshed tears to her eyes. It hurt to think of leaving, of trying to return to the peaceful life she'd enjoyed before her cousin's untimely death.

That trip had changed everything. Things would never return to the old normal. Never. Not only had she lost Vicki, she had essentially lost her best male friend, the guy she had admired for most of her life. In leaving behind their casual, amiable relationship, they had effectively broken that bond without establishing another connection in its place. Was it too late? Perhaps not.

Sara cuddled the armful of wriggly kittens for solace. "Adam?"

He answered without turning. "Yes?"

"What do you want to do when all this is over?"

He shrugged. "Meaning?"

"Meaning, do you think we can ever go back to the way things used to be?"

"Not in a million years," he said, sounding gruff.

When he refused to elaborate or even meet her gaze she was at a loss. Her question had been his cue to allude to a happier future, perhaps one in which they became a couple. But he hadn't. Should she? Sara held back for fear his plans did not include her. What she wanted to ask was, "If we can't go back, can we go forward?" but the words refused to come out.

Truth to tell, now that the Texans were in custody, she should return to Paradise. She would as soon as she had a home to go to. Penitent, Sara did say, "I'm sorry I've been underfoot for so long. Cynthia is working on getting the house repaired. There's a chance I can move in there until the cleanup crews get through repainting my old apartment on the square."

Again, Adam sounded irritated. "Have I asked you to leave?"

"No, but…"

He whirled, glaring as if angry. "Look, Sara, the sheriff may be sure the danger has passed but I'm not convinced. You can stay here with us for as long as it takes to wind up the case, okay?"

Taken aback she scowled at him. "Sheriff Caruthers seems convinced it's all over. He's arrested everybody who came up here with Hector. Do you think they'll send more people?"

"Maybe they already have." Adam's purposeful strides toward her caused her to set aside the kittens and rise. When he began listing the various attacks that had occurred, she started to see his point.

"Just because a criminal denies committing a crime, that doesn't mean they didn't do it," Sara argued.

"Why admit to some things and not all?"

"I don't know. Maybe Hector didn't keep close tabs on the others and they acted on their own. Has the sheriff thought of that?"

"He didn't say."

"Well, when we give him the bracelet I found, maybe that will connect it to the girl they arrested. Even if there isn't any human DNA after the cats chewed it, she might admit it's hers. That would put her here in the barn and confirm her admission of guilt about tying up Kurt."

"I would like to know why they went that far, then bailed," Adam said. "I'll call and tell him what we found. Unless he's in a hurry for it, we can take it to town first thing in the morning. I need to stop in to see Will at the bank, too. A personal visit may encourage him to face Helen."

"Will's afraid to face her? That doesn't sound like him," Sara said, frowning. "Of course, considering the way she went ballistic when we ran into her in the store, he may have a good excuse."

"That's why we're not going to their house," Adam explained. "I want you to stay as far from Helen as possible."

"You won't get any argument from me." A shiver danced up her spine and the hair at the nape of her neck tingled. "If she hadn't been hospitalized for exhaustion when my tires were slashed and my apartment painted red, I might think she was to blame."

Sara saw Adam start as if he'd received an electric shock from a cattle prod. He scowled. "Are you sure?"

"Positive. I heard she'd been treated and looked it up, just to be certain."

"So, it did occur to you that the Babcocks could be harassing you, too."

"Of course. Particularly after Helen attacked me at the store. But like I said, she couldn't have done it." Watching Adam's expression she added, "And I don't think Will did it, either, okay? He's a banker, for one thing. He has his career and reputation to consider."

"All right. If we assume you're right, that means the last three Texans taken into custody drugged the dogs and tied up Kurt."

"Works for me."

"Not for me. It doesn't explain who or what frightened them enough to run off."

Sara's mouth felt like cotton. She struggled to swallow. "Maybe they heard us coming home."

"Not according to my brother. He's sure they'd been gone for hours before we found him."

"If the gang heard someone coming then Kurt must have, too. What did he say about it?"

"Just that he overheard muffled arguing. At first he thought it was coming from the same people who had taped him up. Later, after they'd gone, he suspected otherwise."

"That's it? That's all?"

"Yeah." Adam shrugged again. "Come on. Let's go in the house. Mrs. K says she's not coming back until the dust settles and it's my turn to make supper."

Sara followed him but she wasn't happy about the way he'd abruptly diverted their conversation. First he'd suggested more enemies, then he'd left her in limbo with no idea who her additional nemeses might be.

Knowing your enemies was bad enough. Imagining additional threats around every corner and hidden in every shadow was nearly enough to drive her 'round the bend, as locals like to say. She was just plain tired. Tired of being scared. Tired of making excuses for innocent past actions. Tired of visualizing Vicki's last breaths. And tired of wondering what was going to happen with regard to Adam.

If she could be certain they'd come out of this mess unscathed and ready to start a new life—together—she knew she'd be able to cope with just about anything. Any enemy. Any nameless, faceless evil.

But she didn't know that, did she? Adam used to be a solicitous friend who had hugged and touched her without qualm. Now, he seemed to be avoiding her. And she missed him. He could be standing right next to her and she'd still miss him as long as he continued to act so aloof.

Take my hand. Circle my shoulders with your strong arms. Guide me as we walk together. You don't have to kiss me again. Just be with me, she thought, wishing she were brave enough to say all that aloud.

Swiveling her head she scanned the yard between the back of the house and the barn. To her dismay, she almost wished some new threat would appear, something that would trigger Adam's protective instincts once more and cause him to draw her closer.

And then she realized how illogical she was being. To wish for danger was to complain about the divine guardianship she'd been receiving all along. She didn't really want to manipulate Adam; she merely wanted him to go back to being her concerned friend. Or did she?

Sara almost snorted in disgust. Prayers that Adam would stop viewing and treating her like an old buddy had been answered. She'd gotten *exactly* what she had asked for.

I'm sorry, Father, she prayed silently. *I was wrong about Adam. I was wrong about everything. Give me my friend back. Please?*

An unexpected gust of icy wind blew in from the

northwest and made her shiver. She glanced at the sky and noted a new gathering of dark clouds. Her first thought was that nature was setting the scene for another attack. Or warning her that one was imminent. But that notion was foolish. Wasn't it?

Pausing two steps below Adam as he opened the kitchen door, Sara wondered if her imagination was running away with her or if she was truly still in danger. Her skin crawled. The fine hair on her arms prickled.

Even the farm dogs were acting odd. Some circled the porch. Others sniffed the air as if they were expecting something. One began to bark, triggering all the others to join in.

That was enough for Sara. She ran up the steps, pushed past Adam and beat him through the door. The trouble was, she didn't stop there. Passing through the living room she pounded up the stairs to her room, shut the door and whipped the curtains closed.

Now that she was safe in the darkening room she felt foolish. She also wasn't ready to come out and go back downstairs. Not when she might be asked to explain herself.

It hardly mattered whether her actions were based on a flesh-and-blood enemy or on her confusion about her relationship with Adam. Either way, all she wanted to do was pull the bedcovers over her head and hide like a frightened child.

That wasn't the way people of faith met challenges, she lectured herself as she stood there alone. Scripture said if God was for her, no one could stand against her. So why did she feel as if her whole world was about to implode?

The only prayer she managed was, "God, help me."

TWENTY-ONE

Adam asked his brother to fetch Sara at suppertime. The ploy worked. She joined them for the meal. Conversation was so stilted and sparse, however, the tension was palpable.

Kurt did most of the talking, finally asking, "So, what's wrong with you two? Did you have a fight or something?"

Sara said, "No," while Adam merely shook his head.

"Great. Whatever." Kurt scraped up the last of his potatoes and leftover chicken, pushed back from the table and took his plate to the sink. When the farm dogs began a fresh chorus he looked out the window. "We have company."

Adam was on his feet immediately, hand and arm extended in a silent order for Sara to stay where she was. It didn't surprise him that she moved. What was a surprise was who their visitor turned out to be.

"It looks like Will Babcock," Kurt said.

Sara pushed in beside him to peer out. "Really? Maybe he brought the journal."

"I told him to take it to the sheriff," Adam grumbled, slamming out the back door and jogging to the fancy truck that had stopped between the house and barn.

Another surprise awaited him there. Will had brought his mother along.

Adam nodded at her to be polite, then focused on Will. "Did you get it?"

"Yes." Will stepped out and passed a slim notebook to Adam.

As he did so, Helen sat still as a statue, eyes forward, spine stiff. Adam knew he should invite them in for coffee but ignored pleasantries. The last thing they needed was for Helen to lose control and attack Sara again. It was bad enough that Will had brought her in the first place.

"I think I found the references you wanted," Will said. "Mother understands that it will help convict the men who hurt my sister."

Glancing past him, Adam studied Helen. She seemed to be coping. She looked stalwart but not violent. Will was speaking but between the barking of the dogs and thunder booming from the clouds, it was hard to hear what he had to say.

Will winced as lightning flashed. "Can we go in for a second so I can show you?"

Adam wanted to deny the request. Once he and Sara had a chance to read Vicki's thoughts for themselves they would surely come to the same conclusions. So would the sheriff. Nevertheless, he supposed it wouldn't hurt if Will stepped into the kitchen. Seeing and interacting with him might actually soothe Sara. Besides, only fools stood outside when there was a thunderstorm in the offing.

Adam eyed the truck, hoping Will understood his unspoken question.

He did. "Mom wants to stay out here. She just came along to keep an eye on this." He tapped the hard cover of the journal. "It was the only way she'd let me take it out of the house."

"You know who else is inside, right?"

Will turned away from his mother and nodded. "I know. And I want to apologize to her, too."

"All right." Adam led the way. "If you're sure Helen will be okay out here by herself. It's fixing to rain."

"We talked about that on the drive out here. She isn't ready to socialize but she'll be safe and dry in the cab of the truck. I thought it would do her good to be part of the solution to the mystery of my sister's passing."

Drops the size of nickels were beginning to dot the porch. Adam opened the door and gave it a push. "After you."

Sara stayed by the sink, leaning against the counter for support. Since Adam had obviously invited Will in, he must think it was for the best, yet she had misgivings.

Will didn't smile but he did nod to her. "Sara. I want you to know how sorry I am for blaming you. I finally read every word my sister wrote for myself. It's clear other forces were at work—providing her death wasn't accidental the way we first thought."

Her lips were dry, her throat constricted with emotion. She managed to say, "Thank you," before tears choked away more words.

The men carried the familiar journal to the kitchen table and opened it. Will pointed. "Here. And here. She even names names, although she says the proof is hidden in some office, wherever that is."

Sara cleared her throat. "It was washed away in the flood. That's why Vicki insisted on going out that night. She wanted to bring back the signed receipts. I tried to talk her out of it." Again, her voice broke.

"We know," Adam said flatly. "Let me read this, then we'll talk about it."

Rather than be upset, Sara was thankful for his interruption. Retelling that awful night made the loss fresh, made her ache almost as badly as she had at the time. Instead of arguing, she took a couple of deep, settling breaths and thanked God for the answers they were now receiving. The criminals could be prosecuted. Vicki's findings would help prove their guilt and they'd be sent to prison. Hopefully, even more of them would pay the price than were currently cooling their heels in the tiny Paradise jail.

A new calm enveloped her, wrapping her in a cocoon of healing and pouring warmth over her head in a soothing cascade of peace. Soon all her trials would be over. The threats would be removed and she could go back to the uncomplicated life she'd once taken for granted.

Sara smiled to herself. And when she did go home, she wouldn't be alone. She'd have a new pet. One of the darling striped kittens would go with her. So sweet. So precious and cuddly—when they kept their claws sheathed.

The smile widened. Sighing with contentment she turned toward the kitchen window and imagined those beautiful, blue-eyed babies tucked in between their favorite bales of hay.

Eyes wide she blinked, disbelieving. Gasped. *No! No!* It couldn't be. She had to be hallucinating. Her jaw dropped open. Choking, gulping air, she pointed. Seconds later she managed to yell, "Fire!"

Adam was moving before the others finished processing the warning. He shouted, "Call 9-1-1," to Kurt as he burst out the door, sailed off the porch and splashed through the rain and mud toward the glow.

There was one fire extinguisher mounted by the entrance and another back where they kept the tack. A quick assessment told him that the second unit was already inaccessible. Adam grabbed the closer one, inverted it and started to attack the base of the fire.

That hotspot was almost out when he noticed other starts within the wooden structure. This was no accidental fire. This was arson. How many gang members had they missed arresting?

Continuing to beat back the flames he shouted to Kurt, "Get the horses out! I'll try to hold this."

Kurt snapped lead ropes on two mares' halters and started to lead them to safety. Adam saw him pass those leads to Will as soon as the flames were behind them, then go back for more.

Will? Helen! Where was Helen? Will Babcock was in the clear because he'd been in the house. Had his mother been sitting in his truck when they'd run past just now? Adam had been so focused on putting out the fire he hadn't noticed.

Kurt started to pass him again, leading a mare with a foal. The baby panicked and ran the wrong way, scattering chickens and making his dam go berserk. Kurt hung onto the rope. The mare reared, lifting him off the ground.

Knowing that the extinguisher was nearly out of chemicals and there was no possible way he could get the fire under control by himself, Adam tossed it aside and went to his brother's aid. He smacked the mare on her rump and she ran for safety with her foal and a flock of hens at her heels.

"How many more?" Adam shouted.

"Two!"

"Okay, you take the stallion." A brief glance out the door showed Sara, her hair plastered down by rain, holding on to the mare's halter and trying to soothe her as she urged her and the foal farther away.

Gratitude toward God swelled, bringing more tears to Adam's stinging eyes than the smoke already had. A barn could be rebuilt. Loved ones were irreplaceable. When all this was over...

"I got 'em both," Kurt shouted. He passed one of the lead ropes to his brother. "Let's get out of here!"

Adam was all for that. Some fires were impossible to defeat, even when professionals tackled them. Had he had his engine and enough water at the outset, he figured he could have squelched the flames. By now, it was too late to save the barn.

Sirens in the distance gave him some hope. So did the rain. It had become a deluge, pounding the metal roof as if a hundred men with hammers were up there swinging as hard and as fast as they could. He hurried out the door to where everyone else waited.

Suddenly, a figure passed him at a run and disappeared into the billowing smoke. He wouldn't have been positive who it was if he hadn't heard her screech, "My kittens!"

Sara had been in the barn often enough to navigate it blind. She knew to stay low, as much beneath the layer of smoke as possible. It wasn't necessary to crawl—yet— but it wouldn't be long before the good air near the floor was all there was left.

She made straight for the hidey-hole, hoping the kittens hadn't fled deeper into the stack where she'd never find them in time. Coughing, she bent to reach into the slit, mindless of scratches from the dry stems. Her fingers touched softness. She hooked two fingers around the kitten's head and gently lifted, the way its mother would. That one she tucked into a jacket pocket for safekeeping while she probed again.

"Come on, babies. You know me. Please?" she cooed,

reaching and patting with her hand. A paw? Was that a paw? It had withdrawn but she was certain it had been there. Dropping to her knees with her chest lying on the lowest bale, she reached as far as she could. Normally she wouldn't have grabbed the kitten by one leg but this was a matter of life and death.

Sara hauled it out, set it on the bale so they were nose to nose and reassured it gently. "That's right, baby. You're okay. Come on. Let's go in my pocket with your brother or sister."

Except two wouldn't fit securely, she discovered, transferring the second little cat to the opposite side and hoping both would stay put until she located the third.

Once again she bent down. Something tangled in her wet hair. Yanked so hard she yelped. "Ow!"

What in the world? Was she caught on a hay hook or some other discarded tool? Sara twisted and reached for her scalp.

There was a hand clenched there; bony fingers that felt like the talons of a bird of prey. Only it wasn't. It was human. And the human was screaming as if being scorched by the encroaching flames.

Sara grabbed the wrist. Held as tightly as she could and lurched up toward it, putting her whole body behind the move. She heard a crack. The fingers released her. Now her assailant was howling.

Strong hands grabbed Sara's shoulders from behind and lifted her. She struggled. "No!"

Through reddened, smarting eyes she saw Will picking up his mother. Adam had hold of Sara. He swung her into his arms and whirled, racing for the door in a bent-over stance.

All she could think of was the last kitten. As soon as Adam set her on her feet outside the burning barn she checked her pockets and withdrew the two she had rescued. "There's one more," she wailed, focusing on Adam. "I didn't get them all!"

His hesitation was brief. In moments he had spun and reentered the barn. The fire had reached the rafters by now and was licking out the top of the door with red and orange tongues of superheated flame.

Sara gasped. "Adam!" What had she done? He'd never have taken a chance like that if she hadn't yelled at him.

Behind her, a Paradise fire engine was engaging their pump. Firefighters in full gear ran toward the fire. A nozzle blossomed, showering the open door with a mist that steamed and sizzled, fogging the interior.

"Adam!" Sheltering the kittens inside her jacket Sara wept openly. Every thought was of the man she loved, every word an echo of his name. "A-dam!"

He couldn't be gone. Not her Adam. Not when she had finally admitted how much she loved him. At that moment it didn't matter whether he loved her or not. All she wanted was to see him again, to know he had survived.

Tears clouded her vision. She lifted her face to heaven and let the rain wash away her weeping as she clasped her hands and silently pled for his life.

Smoke was replaced by the steam as firefighters continued to shower the open doorway. A shadow moved. Took shape. It was Adam. He was staggering but alive.

Sara was literally sobbing. He was not only alive—he had the last kitten in his capable hands.

EPILOGUE

There was a celebration of sorts in the hospital ER, with Adam as guest of honor. Four others were also treated for smoke inhalation. Will and Helen were in separate rooms. Kurt and Sara had been allowed to join Adam for debriefing.

Adam sat up and attempted to talk. He ended up coughing, so Sara stepped in to explain to Sheriff Caruthers. "Helen Babcock set the fire," she said. "Will had left her out in the truck while he came inside to show us Vicki's journal. She'd fooled him into believing she was mentally okay because she was willing to let him bring it over and share it."

Caruthers frowned. "What caused her to get so irrational all of a sudden?"

"That's the key. It wasn't sudden. Remember the vandalism the Texans denied? They were telling the truth. Helen was behind most of it. Will only came along to try to keep her from really hurting anyone. He was the one who lit the flare out at the accident, but it was Helen who got it away from him and threw it at my car."

"The red paint, too?"

"Helen," Sara said sadly. "Will got there too late to stop her. That was how his boot print ended up in the apartment. She'd flattened my tires already so he hustled her out of there as fast as he could. He's not sure how she managed to sneak back and leave the threatening note on my windshield at the repair garage, but we assume that was her doing, too."

Caruthers was shaking his head. "I don't know where she got the strength to break up the furniture in the second place," he said. "Did Will do that?"

"To keep her from setting it on fire, instead," Adam choked out, triggering another spate of coughing.

"He was trying to get professional help for her," Sara interjected. "She refused to see a doctor and he kept hoping he'd be able to handle her himself, especially if he could convince her that the journal proved Vicki didn't die due to my negligence. I guess he was wrong."

The sheriff closed his notebook. "Okay. That'll do for now. You folks take it easy. I'm gonna go talk to the Babcocks."

Kurt followed him out, leaving Sara and Adam alone. She sat down next to him and reached for his hand, relieved when he didn't pull away. "The next time I ask you to do something for me, feel free to refuse. You almost got yourself killed rescuing that kitten."

He gave her a lopsided smile. "Hey, I'm a sucker for a pretty face and big blue eyes."

Blushing, Sara chuckled softly. "It's about time you paid the right kind of attention to me."

Adam laughed, turned away to cough, then laughed some more. "I was talking about the kitten but you're not bad to look at, either, sweetheart."

Her grin widened. "Thanks, cowboy. Does this mean you're through pushing me away?"

"That was for your own good. You were an emotional

wreck. I couldn't be sure your feelings weren't being influenced by everything else that had happened."

"Of course they were," she shot back. "I realized how short life can be. I wanted to make the most of every moment."

"Oh, yeah?" He brought her fingertips to his lips and kissed them.

Sara practically melted from the tenderness, from the look in his glistening eyes. The closest he had come to that same expression before was when he had kissed her as a pretense. No amount of imagination could have created the affection she was seeing now. It was time to speak up.

"I love you, Adam."

He gave her a lazy, crooked smile. "I love you, too. I hope you're not saying that just because I risked my life to rescue your helpless kitty."

"It's definitely a good start," she replied, leaning closer.

"I'm only a regular guy trying to do the best he can with the skills he was given," Adam said. "Will that be good enough for you?"

Sara moved in until she was whispering against his lips. "More than good enough. It always has been."

And then he kissed her.

* * * * *

If you loved this book,
be sure to pick up these books from
Valerie Hansen's miniseries
The Defenders

Nightwatch
Threat Of Darkness
Standing Guard
A Trace Of Memory
Small Town Justice

Available now from Love Inspired Suspense!

Find more great reads at
www.LoveInspired.com

Dear Reader,

Not all friends make good mates. Not all mates make good friends. The person who can find both qualities in one person is truly blessed.

In this story, Sara was assuming unkind thoughts in the minds of others and she was often wrong, yet she based her reactions on those perceptions because she blamed herself for a tragedy. That's easy to do when we experience the loss of someone we love. I believe one secret to reclaiming joy is in giving thanks for what we once had, even though it's now lost, and embracing the future as the gift it truly is.

There are plenty of trials in daily life that we can't cope with on our own. There is nothing God can't handle once we decide to let go and trust Him.

You can reach me via email: val@valeriehansen.com.

Blessings,
Valerie Hansen

Get 4 FREE REWARDS!

We'll send you 2 FREE Books plus 2 FREE Mystery Gifts.

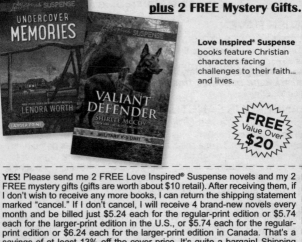

Love Inspired® Suspense books feature Christian characters facing challenges to their faith... and lives.

FREE Value Over $20

SPECIAL EXCERPT FROM

SUSPENSE

When criminal lawyer Tyler Everson witnesses a murder, he becomes the killer's next target—along with his estranged wife, Annabelle, and their daughter. Now they need to enter witness protection in Amish country.

Read on for a sneak preview of
Amish Haven *by Dana R. Lynn,*
the exciting conclusion of the Amish Witness Protection miniseries, available March 2019 from
Love Inspired Suspense!

Annie was cleaning up the dishes when the phone rang. She didn't recognize the number.

"Hello?"

"Annie, it's me."

Tyler.

Her estranged husband. The man she hadn't seen in two years.

"Annie? You there?"

She shook her head. "Yes, I'm here. It's been a frazzling day, Tyler. What do you want?"

A pause. "Something's happened last night, Annie. I can't tell you everything, but the US Marshals are involved. I'm being put into witness protection."

"Witness protection? Tyler, people in those programs have to completely disappear."

In her mind, she heard Bethany ask when she would see her daddy again.

"I know. It won't be forever. At least I hope it won't. I need to testify against someone. Maybe after that, I can go back to being me."

A sudden thought occurred to her. "Tyler, the reason you're going into witness protection… Would it affect me at all?"

"What do you mean?"

"Someone was following me today."

"Someone's following you?" Tyler exclaimed, horrified.

"You never answered. Could the man following me be related to what happened to you?"

"I don't know. Annie, I will call you back." He disconnected the call and went down the hall.

Marshal Mast was sitting at a laptop in an office at the back of the house. He glanced up from the screen as Tyler entered. "Something on your mind, Tyler?"

"I called my wife to tell her I was going into witness protection. She said she and my daughter were being followed today."

At this information, Jonathan Mast jumped to his feet. "Karl!"

Feet pounded in the hallway. Marshal Karl Adams entered the room at a brisk pace. "Jonathan? Did you need me?"

"Yes, I need you to make a trip for me. What's the address, Tyler?"

Tyler recited the address. Would Karl and Stacy get there in time? How he wished he could go with him…

Don't miss
Amish Haven *by Dana R. Lynn,*
available March 2019 wherever
Love Inspired® Suspense books and ebooks are sold.

www.LoveInspired.com

Looking for inspiration in tales
of hope, faith and heartfelt romance?

Check out **Love Inspired**® and
Love Inspired® **Suspense** books!

New books available every month!

SPECIAL EXCERPT FROM

Love Inspired®

*Finally following his dreams of opening a bakery,
Caleb Hartz hires Annie Wagler as his assistant.
But they both get more than they bargain for when his
runaway teenage cousin and her infant son arrive.
Can they work together to care for mother and child—
without falling in love?*

Read on for a sneak preview of
The Amish Bachelor's Baby *by Jo Ann Brown,
available February 2019 from Love Inspired!*

"I wanted to talk to you about a project I'm getting started on. I'm opening a bakery."

"You are?" Annie couldn't keep the surprise out of her voice.

"*Ja,*" Caleb said. "I stopped by to see if you'd be interested in working for me."

"You want to hire me? To work in your bakery?"

"I've had some success selling bread and baked goods at the farmers' market in Salem. Having a shop will allow me to sell year-round, but I can't be there every day and do my work at the farm. My sister Miriam told me you'd do a *gut* job for me."

"It sounds intriguing," Annie said. "What would you expect me to do?"

"Tend the shop and handle customers. There would be some light cleaning. I may need you to help with baking sometimes."

"*Ja*, I'd be interested in the job."

"Then it's yours. If you've got time now, I'll give you a tour of the bakery, and we can talk more about what I'd need you to do."

"Gut." The wind buffeted her, almost knocking her from her feet.

She mumbled that she needed to let her twin, Leanna, know where she was going. He wrapped his arms around himself as another blast of wind struck them.

"Hurry…anna…" The wind swallowed the rest of his words as she rushed toward the house.

She halted midstep.

Anna?

Had Caleb thought he was talking to her twin? She'd clear everything up on their way to the bakery. She wanted the job. It was an answer to so many prayers, for God to let her find a way to help her sister be happy again, happy as Leanna had been before the man she loved married someone else without telling her.

Leanna was attracted to Caleb, and he'd be a fine match for her. Outgoing where her twin was quiet. A well-respected, handsome man whose *gut* looks would be the perfect foil for her twin's. But Leanna would be too shy to let Caleb know she was interested in him. That was where Annie could help.

As she was rushing to the house, she reminded herself of one vital thing. She must be careful not to let her own attraction to Caleb grow while they worked together.

That might be the hardest part of the job.

Don't miss
The Amish Bachelor's Baby *by Jo Ann Brown,*
available February 2019 wherever
Love Inspired® *books and ebooks are sold.*

www.LoveInspired.com

Inspirational Romance to Warm Your Heart and Soul

Join our social communities to connect with other readers who share your love!

Sign up for the Love Inspired newsletter at **www.LoveInspired.com** to be the first to find out about upcoming titles, special promotions and exclusive content.
